MAGIC & MYSTERY

STARRY HOLLOW WITCHES, BOOK 2

ANNABEL CHASE

RED PALM PRESS LLC

Magic & Mystery

Starry Hollow Witches, Book 2

By Annabel Chase

Sign up for my newsletter here http://eepurl.com/ctYNzf **and like me on** Facebook **so you can find out about new releases**.

Cover Design by Alchemy

❀ Created with Vellum

CHAPTER 1

"Sweet baby Elvis, stop contemplating the state of the universe and pick a spot," I said, my patience wearing thin.

Prescott Peabody III, my nine-year-old Yorkie, looked up at me with a blank expression.

"This is the fifth patch of grass you've rejected," I complained. "Why are they not good enough for your poop?"

It was like *Waiting for Godot* sometimes when I took PP3 out for a walk. His Royal Canine had definite ideas about which blades of grass were worthy of his feces. I'd blame our newfound affluence, except he was like this back in New Jersey, too.

As I impatiently awaited the not-so-grand finale of our walk, I surveyed the estate surrounding us. Behind us stood Rose Cottage, the charming house where my parents had lived and where I'd been born. Thornhold, the ancestral home where my aunt and cousin lived, stood in the distance. I still couldn't believe I lived in a place as incredible as this. And I still couldn't believe that a paranormal town like Starry Hollow existed. Until my arrival here, my travel had been limited to the New Jersey Turnpike and the shore, and my exposure to witches had been limited to multiple viewings of *The Wizard of Oz*. It had come as quite a shock to learn that I came from a long, distinguished line of witches and wizards.

My cousin Aster approached on foot, dressed in a stark white pantsuit and statement jewelry. She was the youngest of the Rose-Muldoon siblings, and the most like her mother —the formidable Hyacinth Rose-Muldoon.

"Oh, good. At least you're alone," she said.

I glanced down at the indecisive dog at my feet. "Not entirely."

She ignored PP3. As a witch, she was partial to cats. "I made the mistake of dropping in to see Florian in the main house."

"What's wrong with that?"

She rolled her eyes. "He had a...friend over. He really needs to place a protective spell on the door when he's entertaining guests."

"Or you could try knocking," I suggested.

She blew a dismissive raspberry. "Thornhold is not his bachelor playground, no matter how many toys and games he tries to cram into his man cave." She glanced around the grounds. "Where's Marley?"

"My ambitious ten year old is in the cottage, trying to decipher the runes I've been drawing."

Aster flashed those perfect pearly whites. "Ah, runes. How are your lessons coming along?"

"I have runecraft again this week with Hazel, plus some lady called Marigold is coming by tomorrow."

"Marigold?" Aster echoed. "I suppose it's for your psychic skills assessment. I heard Mother mention it to someone on the phone."

"Psychic skills?" I asked. "What's that?"

"I'll leave it to Marigold to explain," Aster said. "So listen,

Mother and I agree that it would be a good idea if you got involved with some of the nonprofits in town. Since I'm involved in several of them, I thought I'd invite you along to a meeting or two."

"What kind of nonprofits?"

"There are a variety to choose from," she said. "I'm the chairwoman of the VWFF…"

"The Volkswagen Fahrvergnugen?"

Aster shot me a quizzical look. "The Vampires Without Fangs Foundation. The vampires involved are lovely, so that might be a good place to start."

I scrunched my nose. "You're the chairwoman of a vampire foundation? Why?"

"My father founded the organization fifty years ago and a Rose has been chairing it ever since."

"The vampires don't find that patronizing? Can't they take care of their own fangless vampires?"

Aster patted my hand. "You need to learn to be more civic-minded, Ember. Vampires missing their fangs is not simply a vampire problem. It's a problem for everyone."

"Why?" It seemed to me that vampires without fangs were less of a problem than vampires *with* fangs, at least from the point of view of other paranormals.

"There are other organizations, if that one doesn't interest you," Aster said. "There's…"

"Let me guess," I interjected. "Fairies Without Wings? Elves Without Pointy Ears?"

Her mouth formed a thin line. "I'm sure you think it's very funny, but you try being a fairy without wings. It's demoralizing."

I put on my serious face. "Okay, I'm listening. Tell me the other options." PP3 hopped around me, tangling his leash around my legs.

Aster began to tick off the list. "The Home for Wayward

Paranormals, the Senior Citizens of Starry Hollow, the Starry Hollow Tourism Board."

"That last one," I said. What better way to learn about the town than to volunteer to promote it?

She clapped her hands together. "Oh, good. That's one of my favorites, too." She pulled out her phone and checked her calendar. "The next meeting is Thursday at seven. I'll pick you up promptly at six forty-five."

"I'll need to make arrangements with Mrs. Babcock to watch Marley," I said.

"Of course. I'm glad you're doing this with me. It's nice to have another Rose to share the responsibility."

I knew what she meant. It was clear that her siblings, Linnea and Florian, didn't carry their weight. From Linnea's point of view, I could understand it. She was a single mom trying to run a busy inn on her own. Florian, on the other hand, had no excuse. He wanted to live the wealthy bachelor lifestyle without taking on any responsibility and his mother enabled him.

"I'll see you at dinner in an hour then," Aster said. "Sterling is bringing the boys over after their piano lesson."

"Dinner?" I repeated.

Aster inclined her head. "Of course. It's Sunday. We always get together for dinner on Sunday. Has no one told you?"

"No one told me."

Aster blew out a breath. "Honestly, I don't know how this family functions sometimes. Sunday dinner is a Rose-Muldoon tradition. You and Marley are expected. After all—"

"We're Roses?"

She smiled. "Why, yes, you are."

I looked down at the bottom of my pants and shoes, splattered with mud. "I guess I'd better go and change, then."

. . .

Sunday dinner was, unsurprisingly, a grand affair. Unlike our first dinner at Thornhold, however, all the children were included this time—Linnea's teenaged children, Bryn and Hudson, and Aster's twin boys, four-year-old Ackley and Aspen. Sterling sat between them, presumably to keep them from causing mischief in front of their no-nonsense grandmother.

"It's so nice to see you all together," Aunt Hyacinth said. "Maybe one of these days we'll be able to add three more chairs to the table."

"Mother," Linnea said in a warning tone.

I wasn't sure what she meant.

"Oh, Linnea," Aunt Hyacinth said lightly. "You know I only have your best interest at heart. I want to see all my offspring happily coupled. Never mind your first marital mistake."

Ah. Now I understood. She wanted 'appropriate' partners for Florian and Linnea.

"Who's the third chair for?" Florian asked.

Aunt Hyacinth smiled at me. "Why, Ember's partner, of course. Her father would have wanted to see her settle down with a nice wizard in Starry Hollow."

That was doubtful, since my father had never intended for me to live in Starry Hollow. The whole reason I was here now was a fluke. My daughter and I had been living a perfectly normal life in Maple Shade, New Jersey, when an unfortunate encounter with a mobster triggered my magic and set off a beacon that alerted the Rose-Muldoon family to my existence. Thankfully for me, they arrived when they did, because Marley and I were nearly burnt to a crisp by a mobster madman. James Litano, otherwise known as Jimmy the Lighter, was a known pyromaniac, and he'd been determined to exact revenge on me for repossessing his car. So now Marley and I lived in Starry Hollow, the paranormal town where I'd been born and where my mother had died.

"I think the table seems crowded enough," thirteen-year-old Hudson said. "I barely have any elbow room as it is." He jostled his elbow for good measure, deliberately knocking it into his sister's arm.

"Hey," Bryn snapped. "Keep your bony body to yourself, Skeletor."

"That's enough, you two," Linnea said in a low voice.

I had no doubt that manners were critical at Sunday dinners. Everyone wanted to put on a good show for the grand matriarch, Hyacinth Rose-Muldoon.

"There is always more room at the table here," Aunt Hyacinth said. "This table is imbued with magic, Hudson. It will expand without the need for an insert."

Well, that was handy.

Aunt Hyacinth rang her little silver bell and platters began to float into the room like a weightless parade. My empty glass suddenly filled with an amber liquid that I didn't recognize.

"What's this?" I asked, lifting my glass to inspect it.

"Honeysuckle bizzbeer," Florian said. "It happens to be one of my favorites."

"Mother chooses each of our favorite drinks in rotation," Aster explained. "This week is Florian's turn."

"Why does everyone have to have the same drink?" I asked. "If you can fill your glass with whatever magical liquid you like, what's the point?"

Aunt Hyacinth settled her gaze on me. "It's called manners, dear. And we shall be working on yours, have no doubt."

My first inclination was to argue, but I opted to remain silent. Aunt Hyacinth had been nothing short of generous

6

since our arrival and I wasn't foolish enough to deliberately annoy her.

I tasted the amber liquid and was surprised to find it smooth and refreshing. "Does it do anything to me?"

Hudson laughed. "Sure. If you drink enough of them, they'll make you drunk."

"Hudson," Linnea said sharply.

"What do you think it would do?" Florian asked with a smirk. "Turn you into a toad or something?" He took a sip from his own glass and, that quickly, he was gone.

"Florian," Aunt Hyacinth said in a no-nonsense tone. "You know better than to do magic at the table. You're worse than a child."

"He *is* a child," Aster grumbled.

"Mom," Marley said excitedly. "He's still here."

He was still where? Had he slid under the table? Before I had a chance to peer below deck, a green frog hopped from Florian's chair onto his plate. Someone screamed. I think it was me.

"Florian Rose-Muldoon," Aunt Hyacinth snapped, "this is unacceptable. You turn yourself back this instant. You're setting a bad example for the children."

"Nothing new there," Aster muttered.

The frog hopped on the table in an agitated circle.

"This isn't funny, Florian," Linnea said. "Ember was just asking a question. There's no need to make a point."

The frog's long, powerful tongue shot from its mouth, knocking over Florian's glass. The liquid spilled onto the table and the frog hopped beside it, lapping up tiny drops.

"Well, at least we know it's Florian," Sterling said. Nobody laughed.

Aunt Hyacinth held out her hand. *"Restituere."*

Everyone stared at the frog expectantly. Nothing happened.

Aunt Hyacinth frowned. "You try, Aster. Transformation spells were always your strong suit."

Aster focused her attention on the frog and raised her hand, palm out. "*Reditus.*" The frog blinked back at her.

Aster and her mother exchanged worried looks.

"Why can't you change him back?" Marley asked.

"Someone else must have performed the transformation spell," Aster explained.

"Florian didn't do this to himself," Linnea said. "Someone else has turned him into a frog."

"Cool," Aspen said, staring at his uncle with round eyes. He glanced up at his mother. "Can we keep it?"

"Of course we can keep it," Aster said. "That frog is your uncle. We're not simply going to set him loose in the woods and forget about him."

Aunt Hyacinth looked ready to explode. I don't know how I knew that, since her face remained passive. It must have been the rigid way she held her body as she gazed at her amphibian son. I suddenly felt sorry for the responsible party. That person didn't know what they were in for. Then again, if someone was turning Florian into a frog, they had to know exactly whom they were messing with.

"Someone be so kind as to call the sheriff while I prepare accommodations for Florian," Aunt Hyacinth said. She rang her silver bell, and Simon, her butler, appeared in the doorway with a glass enclosure. Their magical link never ceased to amaze me.

Florian the Frog seemed to know that he was about to be imprisoned. He began to hop across the table, in and out of plates and bowls, scattering food and splashing liquids, much to the children's delight. His frog feet smoothed the stick of butter and kept going.

"Go, uncle Florian! Go!" Ackley cried.

"Someone catch him," Aster said.

"*Rigescunt indutae*," Linnea said, and snapped her fingers. The frog came to a halt and landed on its back with a small thud.

"Be careful lifting him," Aunt Hyacinth said. "If he's too brittle, you could break off his legs."

"Well, I've always been partial to frog legs myself," Sterling said.

Everyone stared at him in abject horror, causing Aster's husband to sink lower in his seat.

"It was only meant as a joke," he said. "Obviously, I have no interest in eating Florian."

"That should go without saying," Aunt Hyacinth said coolly.

Simon carefully lifted Florian the Frog and placed him in the glass enclosure. "I'll be sure to add the necessary accouterments," he said. "That will keep Master Florian comfortable during his stay."

"Thank you, Simon," Aunt Hyacinth said. "I know I can count on you."

Aster placed her phone on the table. "The sheriff is on his way. He said he has some news for us that might help."

"That would be a first," Aunt Hyacinth said.

Linnea shot her a disapproving look. "Mother, need I remind you that Sheriff Nash is the children's uncle?"

"No, you needn't remind me, Linnea," Aunt Hyacinth replied coolly. "I wake up to that unfortunate fact every day."

"I really like Uncle Granger," Bryn said.

"Me, too," Hudson said. "He's funny."

"All right then," Aunt Hyacinth said. "The sheriff will arrive shortly. We should at least finish our meal. No need for dinner to spoil because of an unexpected interruption."

Everyone ate in silence. I think we were all too afraid to say the wrong thing and set off my aunt. Anyone who referred to the frogification of her son as an 'unexpected interruption' was not someone to piss off.

Sheriff Nash arrived by the middle of dessert. "Ooh, burstberry sponge cake. That's one of my favorites."

"Would you care for a slice, Sheriff?" Aunt Hyacinth asked.

"Why would she offer him any?" Marley whispered. "She obviously doesn't want him to say yes."

I placed a hand on her leg to silence her. "I'll explain later."

I waited to see whether Sheriff Nash was smart enough to decline.

"I appreciate your hospitality, but not while I'm on duty," Sheriff Nash said. Everyone at the table seemed to breathe an inward sigh of relief.

"So, what's the news you have to share?" Aster asked.

"Yours is the second case of an unexpected transformation spell," he said. "The other one's also a frog."

Linnea's brow creased. "Who is it?"

"Thom Rutledge," the sheriff replied.

"The incubus?" Sterling asked. "I play cards with him sometimes at the Phoenix Club."

The sheriff nodded. "He was discovered this morning."

"During breakfast?" Ackley asked. "Did it happen at meal time, like Uncle Florian?"

The sheriff's brow lifted. "Well, it did happen during *his* meal time." He ceased to elaborate. I wasn't even sure what an incubus was.

"Children, why don't you finish your dessert in the sunroom?" Aunt Hyacinth proposed.

"Really?" Aspen queried. "You never let us eat in the sunroom."

Sterling shushed him. "Then don't mistake a kelpie for a horse. Just go."

The children grabbed their plates and forks and hurried

away from the table. Marley remained behind, looking to me for guidance.

"You're one of the children, Marley," I said. "You should go, too." Even though I knew Marley wasn't a typical ten-year-old, it seemed like the conversation was about to take a turn that wasn't appropriate for her innocent ears.

"I'm finished with my dessert," Marley said stubbornly.

"Then you can go and watch the other children eat theirs," I said firmly.

Marley finally took her cue and scrambled from the table. Once she was out of earshot, Sheriff Nash sat down in the empty chair beside Linnea.

"Okay, so before you continue," I said, "what's an incubus?"

The sheriff chuckled. "Probably best to explain it to you before you meet one in a bar. That's where they prefer to pick up their meals."

"I like bar food," I said. Calamari. Fully loaded nachos. Yum. "What's wrong with that?"

Aunt Hyacinth took a sip of her drink. I noticed that she'd replaced her glass of honeysuckle bizzbeer with a different cocktail. I guess Florian's favorite was no longer required now that he was a frog.

"An incubus is someone who feeds off sexual desire, as well as the act itself," Linnea said.

"It's really not appropriate dinner table conversation," my aunt said.

"You said you wanted to educate Ember," Linnea said. "We can't just limit it to witchcraft. How would you like it if she started dating an incubus without knowing what he was?"

"So, when you said he was discovered as a frog during his meal time," I began, "are you saying he was found in bed?"

"The fairy cleaning service found him in the morning, tangled in the covers," the sheriff said. "A neighbor saw a woman sneak out in the morning, although he said that wasn't unusual. The woman wore a cloak, so he couldn't describe her beyond her height."

"Two eligible bachelors," Aster mused. "That has to be more than a coincidence."

The sheriff shrugged. "Not necessarily, but given Florian and Thom's track record with women, it's entirely possible that it's a disgruntled former date."

I understood what he meant. Those two sounded like more than eligible bachelors. They were serial heartbreakers.

Sterling whistled. "That's going to be a long list of suspects, Sheriff."

The sheriff cleared his throat. "On that note, which one of you can help me out with Florian's most recent...?"

"Conquests?" Aunt Hyacinth interjected. "That's no trouble. Simon has a list."

All heads jerked toward her.

"A list?" Linnea repeated.

"Naturally," Aunt Hyacinth said, cool as a cucumber. "Do you think I don't keep a record of such things? If some scheming vixen starts making claims, I can verify part of her story. More importantly, if a name appears on the list more than twice, I know to start paying attention."

"Has that happened?" Aster queried.

"Not yet," Aunt Hyacinth replied. "But preparation is the key to success." She rang the silver bell that summoned Simon. Almost immediately, he strode through the doorway, clutching a list of names, and handed it to the sheriff.

Sheriff Nash stared at the paper in his hand, dumbfounded. "Um, thanks. I'll let you know what I find out."

"Do be quick about it, Sheriff," my aunt said. "I expect to be kept fully apprised of any developments. The situation is humiliating at best, and dire at worst."

"Why dire?" I asked. Were they worried about his new diet of flies and mosquitoes?

Everyone exchanged uneasy glances.

"If we don't figure out who cast the spell," Aster said, "then we might not be able to reverse it."

"That means Florian would be doomed to live the rest of his life as a frog," Linnea added.

Suddenly, the Kermit joke I'd been about to make no longer felt appropriate. "Wow. I'm sorry," I said.

"Not as sorry as the magic-using miscreant will be," my aunt said. "It's still early, Sheriff. Plenty of time to squeeze in an interview or two before bed, wouldn't you agree?"

The sheriff's jaw twitched. "No worries, Hyacinth. Deputy Bolan and I are on the case."

"Yes," Aunt Hyacinth drawled, taking a long sip of her drink. "That's precisely what concerns me."

CHAPTER 2

THE MISTRESS-OF-PSYCHIC-SKILLS WAS a petite woman with brown corkscrew curls. As she entered the cottage, I caught a glimpse of her green and black striped tights underneath her silver cloak and cringed. The cloaks were weird enough. I drew the line at butt-ugly tights. She set her satchel on the table with brisk efficiency.

"Good morning, Miss Rose," she said, shrugging off her cloak and flinging it onto the back of the chair. "I'm Marigold and I'll be working with you today. I hope you've had your caffeinated beverage of choice because we'll be doing an assessment and you're going to need all the mental energy you can summon."

"So I've been told." I lifted a pen from the table. "I'm ready to fail."

She frowned. "What do you intend to do with a pen?"

"What you normally do. Mark answers on a test," I said.

"Spell's bells. It's not that kind of test," Marigold said. "Now, sit down and I'll explain."

I sat without protest. For such a petite witch, she had a

commanding presence—part cheerleader and part drill sergeant.

"What do you know about psychic abilities?" Marigold asked.

"Outside of movies and TV?" I tapped my chin thoughtfully. "Alec Hale can read my thoughts if I don't shield them. Apparently, it's a vampire thing."

"Right. Anything else?"

"I can make it rain."

"How often have you done that?"

I hesitated. "Once."

"How do you know you made it happen and that it wasn't a coincidence?" she asked.

Hmm. Good question. "I don't know. I felt it in my bones, that I'd done it. My hands tingled."

"Were you under stress?" she queried.

"You might say that." I was in a burning tow truck with a pyromaniac grinning at me from his front lawn. I'd never forget the sight of Jimmy the Lighter attempting to save his luxury car from repossession and murder me at the same time. A true multitasker.

"Rain is a pretty powerful trick for your first magical effort," Marigold said, and clapped her hands. "That bodes well for you today. Okay, first up, we're going to test for telepathy."

"That's reading minds, like Alec?"

She gave a crisp nod.

"Oh, I can't do that."

She eyed me curiously. "How do you know?"

I laughed. "I'm twenty-eight years old. I think I'd know by now if I could read people's thoughts."

Marigold cocked her head and her curls bounced from the sudden movement. "You've never had an experience where you've had uncanny insight into a person's mind? Maybe caught a fleeting thought?"

I pondered the question. "I read people pretty well. Always have. And I thought I heard Alec's voice in my head when we met." I'd assumed it was his own psychic ability pushing its way into my head. Alec was devastatingly handsome, so I'd also thought it was wishful thinking because he called me attractive, or something to that effect.

"Interesting. We'll start with cards and see what we can learn about your abilities." She pulled a deck from the satchel and began to shuffle. "I'm going to look at a card. I want you to close your eyes and concentrate. Tell me what image you see in your mind's eye."

I straightened and closed my eyes, waiting to see if anything formed. "I see multicolored spots."

"That's because you're squeezing your eyes too tightly," Marigold said. "Try to relax and let the image flow to you."

I took a deep breath and focused. "That can't be right. I see a naked woman." I laughed. "She doesn't look anything like a queen of spades."

"What's a queen of spades?"

My brow creased. "What kind of cards are you using?"

"A standard coven deck," she replied. "I've changed cards now. Keep going. We'll worry about your accuracy at the end."

"I see a moon and stars this time," I said. The image reminded me of the Starry Hollow flag that hung from the pole of Linnea's inn, Palmetto House.

We went through the entire deck and, by the final card, I felt the stirrings of a headache.

"Time for a break," Marigold said.

"A break?" I queried, slumping against my chair. "Aren't we finished yet?"

Marigold patted my hand sympathetically. "That was only the first test, Ember."

"I failed, didn't I? I think my imagination was coming up with all sorts of crazy images just to mess with me."

"There is no pass or fail here," Marigold said. "We're simply measuring your aptitude for certain psychic skills, to see how to best train you."

"And?" I prompted.

"There's definitely potential for telepathy." She shuffled the cards and placed them back in the packet.

I yawned. "So what's next?"

"Have a drink of water, and I'll give you something for your headache before we continue."

I inclined my head. "How do you know I have a headache?"

Marigold suppressed a smile. "I'm the Mistress-of-Psychic-Skills for a reason." The way she said it, she may as well have added 'duh' to the end of her sentence. "And, just for the record, my tights are adorable."

Oops. I went into the kitchen for water and, when I returned, Marigold sprinkled a bronze powder into the glass.

"What's that?" I asked.

"A coven remedy for your pain."

I pinched my nose before I drank, just in case.

Marigold proceeded to set up several objects on the table while I was in the kitchen, including a spoon, a feather, and an apple. I couldn't imagine what she intended to do with those.

"I don't intend to do anything with those," she said, reading my mind. "They're part of your telekinetic assessment."

I sat at the table and folded my hands. "So how does this work? Am I supposed to move them with my mind?"

"Pretty much," Marigold said. "Start with the feather,

since obviously that's the lightest. Focus your will on moving the feather. It doesn't need to fly through the air. Even if you manage to move it a fraction, it shows that you have telekinetic potential."

"What about the fact that I made it rain?" I asked. "Was that evidence of telekinesis?"

Marigold shook her head. "That's a different sort of magic. Very powerful. A sure sign that you're a descendant of the One True Witch."

"So not all Silver Moon witches can control the weather?"

"Absolutely not," Marigold said. "For all my psychic abilities, I couldn't force a single drop of rain to fall from the sky."

Score one for me. "So, what does it mean to focus my will?"

"Your will, as in your desired outcome. Concentrate on the feather. Pour all your focus and attention on moving that feather. Block all other thoughts, all other desires. In this moment, there is only moving the feather."

"Basically, you want me to monotask instead of multitask."

Marigold shrugged. "Whatever works for you. There is no one right way because no two witches have exactly the same set of abilities. Each witch develops her own style of magic over time."

I stared at the feather, giving it my full attention. I blocked out thoughts of Marigold and of PP3 snuggled on the sofa. Of Marley at school, probably educating the teacher on one subject or another. I blocked thoughts of Sheriff Nash in his tight jeans and Alec Hale in his million-dollar suit. The only thing in the world I cared about right now was moving that feather as though my life depended on it.

I watched in amazement as the feather shifted a few centimeters to the left.

"I did it!"

Marigold winced. "Actually, I think I may have breathed a little too close to it. So sorry. Let's try it again."

I huffed. "Are you sure? I didn't see you breathing."

"It isn't something you usually see," Marigold pointed out.

Fair enough. I focused my will again. This time, the feather definitely moved.

"That was not you breathing," I said, slapping my palm flat on the table. "I deliberately moved it to the right this time."

"Now, I'd like you to try bending this spoon," Marigold said, tapping the silver spoon on the table.

"Bend the spoon?" I repeated. "But it's made out of metal."

"So it is," Marigold said. "That shouldn't be a deterrent to trying."

I stared at the spoon. "This feels like it should be more advanced work."

"It is," Marigold said. "And even if you can't do it today, it doesn't mean that you'll never be able to bend it. Remember, we're measuring your aptitude."

I couldn't bend the spoon, no matter how hard I tried.

"'A' for effort. Let's move on," Marigold said. She packed away the spoon, the feather, and the apple.

"What about the apple?" I asked.

She shook her head. "If you can't bend the spoon today, it's highly unlikely you'd be able to move the apple. It's too dense."

"But you think eventually I might be able to do that?"

"Perhaps," Marigold said. "The next test I'd like to try is for astral projection."

"I'm sorry. For what?"

"Astral projection. The ability to separate your consciousness from your physical form."

"You mean like an out-of-body experience?"

"Yes," she replied. "It's a form of telepathy. Some witches are able to travel outside of their physical bodies."

"Seriously? Can you do that?" I had to admit, that sounded like a badass skill.

Marigold straightened. "Let's just assume that I can do most of the items on the list. My experience is what enables me to train others."

"So I'll work with you to develop whichever skills I have an aptitude for?"

"That is your aunt's request."

"It makes sense, though, right? If it turns out I can do all this crazy stuff, you wouldn't want me going haywire like Carrie."

Her expression was blank. "Who's Carrie?"

"You know Carrie...by Stephen King?"

Marigold shook her head.

"You're missing out, Marigold. What do you read for fun?"

"I prefer self-help books and books on gardening."

"You should try Stephen King. Very different from what you're reading."

"Why would I want to read something different?" she queried.

I shrugged. "I don't know. Break out of your comfort zone? Expand your literary horizons?"

"I'll take it under advisement," she replied, unconvinced.

We did the astral projection test, which consisted of me sitting on the sofa and concentrating, as well as tests for clairvoyance and teleportation.

"My cousins can all do teleportation, can't they? That's how they were able to bring Marley and me to Starry Hollow from New Jersey." I tried to remember what they'd said at the time. "They used a magical wormhole, I think."

"Yes, it definitely appears to be a strong Rose trait. I'm

confident that, based on your test results, you'll be able to develop this ability, as well."

"Marley, too?"

"It's difficult to know until she comes into her magic next year."

"Is there any downside to my magic being suppressed all these years? Now that my father's spell has been broken, shouldn't magic be pouring out of me?"

"It seems that his suppression spell was damaged, rather than obliterated," Marigold said. "The more magic you do now, however, the faster the spell will erode. Once your lessons begin in earnest, I expect the spell to break completely."

"Why is everything being introduced to me so slowly then? I thought my aunt wanted my magic in full force."

"There's a danger in too much too fast," Marigold said. "It's best to introduce bits and pieces slowly, so that your body and mind have time to adjust."

That made sense. "So, what's the verdict? Am I a future Mistress-of-Psychic-Skills?"

Marigold laughed cheerfully. "It's quite possible. You're showing signs of aptitude for everything on the list, with the exception of clairvoyance."

"But that's the best one," I said.

"Depends on who you ask," Marigold said. "Some find knowledge of the future to be a heavy burden to bear."

"So wait," I said. "Even astral projection? You think I'm going to be able to do that?"

She nodded. "With the right training, yes. Your aunt will be most pleased. Roses aren't generally known for astral projection, or telepathy, for that matter, outside of the usual psychic links with familiars."

"What about my aunt's psychic connection to Simon?" I asked. "Isn't that telepathy?"

"Not quite," Marigold said. "The silver bells are enchanted. Her connection to Simon is spell-based, rather than organic."

"So why do I have abilities that my cousins don't?"

Marigold gave me a pointed look. "You seem to forget that your mother was a witch, too. Lily had many gifts."

She was right. There was so much focus on being a Rose, it was easy to forget that I was half Hawthorne.

"Did you know her?" I asked. Marigold seemed too young to have crossed paths with my mother.

"She died when I was ten," Marigold said. "I remember it vividly, because there was such an outpouring of grief in the community. The coven donned their black cloaks for weeks afterward. It might comfort you to know that she was much loved in Starry Hollow."

It did. "You said she had many gifts. Do you know what they were?"

"A penchant for psychic skills, to be sure. She also had a strong bond with her familiar." Marley paused and looked at me. "But make no mistake, Ember. You were her greatest gift of all."

CHAPTER 3

MY AUNT BREEZED into the offices of *Vox Populi*, the weekly newspaper she owned and, thanks to her blatant nepotism, my current place of employment. In her arms, she held Precious, her fluffy white familiar. The cat seemed perfectly at ease being carried around town like a grocery bag.

"Hyacinth," Tanya said. The fairy office manager couldn't hide her surprise. "How nice to see you here."

Resident elf Bentley Smith jumped from his seat like someone announced a half-price sale on toys. "Hyacinth, what a welcome diversion."

Aunt Hyacinth paused. "Diversion?" She examined Bentley closely. "Are you in need of a diversion from your duties here, Bentley?"

"No, no," Bentley stammered. "That's not what I meant."

I bit my cheek so as not to laugh.

She gave him a withering look. "I would think a journalist such as yourself would be able to convey what he means via the use of words. I imagine it's in the job description." Precious hissed, punctuating my aunt's reprimand.

The associate editor nearly dissolved into a puddle of humiliation right there on the floor.

"Everything okay, Aunt Hyacinth?" I asked, in an effort to draw attention away from Bentley. As annoying as he was, their interaction was painful to witness.

"Where's Alec?" she demanded, surveying the room.

"Right here," Alec said, appearing out of nowhere, as usual. Despite his six-foot-two frame, the vampire was lighter on his feet than an astronaut in space. "At your service, as always."

"Excellent, my dear," Aunt Hyacinth said, brightening. "Listen, I need you to investigate the frog situation."

Alec's brow furrowed. "The frog situation?"

Aunt Hyacinth shot me a quizzical look. "You didn't tell them?"

I shook my head. "I didn't want to embarrass Florian."

My aunt smiled. "Ember, that's so considerate. I never expected it from you."

Ouch. A smack-handed compliment.

"Two of Starry Hollow's most eligible bachelors have been turned into frogs this week," Aunt Hyacinth continued.

"And Florian is one of them?" Alec asked.

My aunt nodded and stroked her familiar. "It happened during our Sunday dinner. One second he was eating and drinking. The next second he was a frog, hopping around the table. The butter had to be disposed of."

"Is the sheriff looking into it?" Alec asked.

"Of course, which is why I want you to add your investigative journalism skills, as well," Aunt Hyacinth said. "You know how I feel about the sheriff. Werewolves are good for tracking fresh meat, not criminals."

No wonder Linnea had fallen out of her mother's good graces when she'd married a werewolf. It wasn't simply that

Wyatt Nash was a womanizer. Aunt Hyacinth clearly had a chip on her shoulder when it came to shifters.

"We'd be honored to assist you," Alec said. "Who's the other bachelor affected?"

"Thom Rutledge," I replied. "An incubus."

"Is that so?" Alec asked, rubbing his smooth chin. "How interesting."

Aunt Hyacinth hushed her mewing cat. "I expect regular updates."

Alec bowed his head slightly. "Of course. Anything for you."

She patted his chiseled cheek like he was a chubby toddler. "I knew you'd come through for me. You always do." She turned around and flicked her finger, causing the door to swing open. Then she swept out of the room without a backward glance, her bright blue kaftan swishing around her ankles.

Once the door clicked closed behind her, Alec turned to the staff. "I want you both working on this."

"Even me?" I asked.

"Even you, Miss Rose," Alec replied.

"She can talk to the sheriff," Bentley said. "I'll pull together a list of ex-girlfriends for both men."

Alec hesitated. "I think you should handle the sheriff, Bentley. Leave the girlfriends for Miss Rose."

"Actually, the sheriff has a list already," I said. "At least for Florian. My aunt gave it to him on Sunday."

"I see," Alec said, adjusting his cufflinks. "Bentley, request a copy of the list from the sheriff, and then you and Miss Rose can get started on the interviews."

"Why can't Miss Rose...?" Bentley began, but Alec cut him off with a death glare. "Fine," he relented. "I'll call the sheriff."

Alec smoothed the front of his suit jacket. "Very well. Let me know when you identify a solid lead."

"Yes, sir," I said, and saluted him.

He gave me a curious look before disappearing into his office at the back of the room.

"Why doesn't he want me to talk to the sheriff?" I asked. "Do I get on his nerves that much? Is Alec afraid it'll impact the information we get?"

"Something like that," Bentley said vaguely. He dialed a number and handed his phone to Tanya. "You can handle the grunt work."

Tanya begrudgingly accepted the task. "Hello, I'd like to speak with Sheriff Nash, please. This is Tanya from *Vox Populi*."

Ten minutes later, we had the list of former flames for Florian, as well as for Thom Rutledge.

"I'm surprised he's so willing to share the information, considering it's an active investigation," I said.

"It's because of Florian," Bentley said. "He knows Hyacinth will be on a rampage until the case is resolved and her son and heir is no longer green and slimy."

"Their mucous coating makes them slimy," I said. Marley had taught me that fact when she's studied amphibians in third grade.

"Who cares why?" Bentley said with a huff and proceeded to study the list. "Let's start with the most recent ones. Their grudges will be the strongest."

"Are we going to divide and conquer?" I asked. "You take Thom's list and I'll take Florian's?"

"I think we should go together," Bentley said. "At least at first. Make sure you're asking the right questions."

"No way. I know how to ask questions," I snapped. That was how I managed to figure out how Fleur Montbatten died. I discovered the former Maiden of the coven dead in the woods when I'd first arrived in Starry Hollow. It was because of my questioning of suspects that the cause of her death was finally revealed. Alec had told me then that I had the potential to be a decent journalist. It was the first time anyone had told me I'd be a decent anything, so I wasn't willing to let Bentley take that away from me now—associate editor or not. Alec Hale was the editor-in-chief, so it was his opinion I was interested in, and not just because he was hotter than all the James Bonds combined.

"I'll make you a deal," Bentley said. "Whichever one of us identifies the culprit first gets the byline."

"What's a byline?" I asked.

He rolled his eyes. "The name that's credited with writing the story. You really don't know anything, do you?"

"I know how to kick you between the legs in a way that will make you cry in a high-pitched voice," I said. "So I wouldn't say I'm completely ignorant."

Bentley's hand drifted down to cover his private area. "Noted."

I flashed him a saucy smile. "Then we have a deal."

Junie Whitaker was a fairy that worked at a salon called Glitter Me This. Stepping through the doors of the salon, I felt like I'd been transported to a version of Oz on steroids. The interior glowed a golden yellow and I seemed to be slapped in the face by wings and glitter everywhere I turned. I gripped the edge of the reception counter in an effort to calm my brain. The room was sensory overload.

"Welcome to Glitter Me This," the fairy receptionist said. "Do you have an appointment?"

"No," I said. "I work for the newspaper and I'm looking for Junie Whitaker."

"Junie's just finishing with a customer," the receptionist said. "If you'll take a seat, she'll be with you in a moment."

I sat in the lobby with the other waiting customers. The fairy beside me was discussing wing colors with her friend.

"I think I want red, white, and blue glitter today," the fairy said, fluttering her wings. I wasn't sure I'd ever get used to the sight. It was like hanging out with giant insects.

"You had that color scheme last month," the friend said. "I like when you get the fuchsia glitter. You can match that stripe in your hair."

Sure enough, the fairy had a narrow section of hair bedazzled with fuchsia glitter.

"I heard you're looking for me?" a voice said.

I glanced up into the face of a pretty fairy. Curly blond hair crowned her head and her top half was busting at the seams. I spotted a trail of purple glitter in her cleavage. I could understand why Aunt Hyacinth was frustrated with Florian. Even in broad daylight, Junie didn't strike me as the type of date you brought home to Hyacinth Rose-Muldoon.

"Junie?" I asked.

"That's right." She chomped on a piece of gum. "You're from the newspaper?" She blew a giant bubble and sucked it back in.

"I am." I looked around the lobby. "Is there somewhere private that we can talk?"

"Is this about Adeline's car?" she asked. "Because I told her I would get it fixed. She didn't need to go ratting me out. There's no story there."

I blinked. "No, that's not why I'm here."

She placed a hand on her hip, her wings fluttering rapidly. "Is it about the incident at the bank? Because I was just having a bad day. I *told* the bank manager that. It's only bad press for the bank if they make a fuss."

"Junie, if we can talk somewhere privately, I'll tell you why I'm here."

She glanced over her shoulder. "Come on. I know a spot."

I was surprised when she ushered me into the broom closet. There was barely enough room for two people to stand without pressing into each other. The shelf behind me dug into my back.

"Okay, we're somewhere private," Junie said. Her breath smelled like cherries.

"Um, I guess we are." Although it was a little claustrophobic, I soldiered on. "I'm covering a story about eligible bachelors in Starry Hollow being turned into frogs."

Her brown eyes popped and she began to laugh. "Frogs? So, if we kiss them, does that mean they turn into princes?" She wiggled her eyebrows. "If so, point me the way to one. I'll pucker up right now."

Right. "Do you know Florian Rose-Muldoon?"

Her expression immediately soured. "I'm a hot fairy. Of course I know Florian."

"He's been turned into a frog."

"That one I'm definitely *not* kissing," she said, folding her arms. "I don't care how much money he has. One night was more than enough."

"So you two dated?"

"That's an exaggeration," she said. "We went out once, a week ago. He took me to Elixir, and then we went back to his place." She sighed. "I'd wanted to see the inside of Thornhold since I was a little girl."

"Was it everything you thought it would be?" I asked. The mansion *was* impressive. I still hadn't managed to visit every room on the main floor.

"I only saw Florian's man cave," she said, scowling. "He refused to show me the rest of the house. Said his mother didn't like him to bring unexpected guests around."

Well, that much was true.

"So the date ended badly?" I queried.

"It ended very well, thank you very much," she said. "For

both of us. But then he didn't call or return any of my text messages." She began to pout. "I thought we'd had a wonderful time."

"Sounds like you did."

"Not wonderful enough, apparently." She bristled. "It was my own fault. I knew better, but I went out with him anyway."

"Do you have any experience with transformation spells?" I asked.

Junie laughed again. "Me? If I were any good with fairy magic, I wouldn't be working here, would I?"

I honestly had no idea.

Suddenly, the door jerked open and I recognized the smirking face of Sheriff Nash.

"Rose?" he queried.

"Rose?" Junie echoed, squinting at me.

"That's my first name," I said quickly. "Rose Marley."

The sheriff rolled his eyes. "May I ask what you're doing in a broom closet with this young fairy?"

"Hey, I'm young, too," I objected.

He heaved a sigh. "It wasn't meant as an insult, Rose."

"Sorry, I just assume everything out of your mouth is meant as an insult."

"You know what they say about assumptions," he said.

"That joke only works when you say 'assume,'" I pointed out. "Assumption doesn't have the letter 'e'"

Junie looked from the sheriff back to me. "Are you two always like this?"

"Like what?" he asked.

"Forget it," Junie said.

"I suppose you're here asking about Florian," the sheriff said. "Why you're in a closet doing it, I have no idea."

"We're not doing it in a closet," I objected.

"You know what I mean," the sheriff said.

"Rose was just telling me about Florian turning into a frog." Junie stifled a laugh. "Serves him right."

"Junie doesn't have experience with transformation spells," I told the sheriff.

"Is that so?" The sheriff gave her an appraising look. "Know anyone who does? I understand there are fairies who accept money for that kind of thing."

She blew air from her nostrils. "If you think for one hot minute that I'd waste my hard-earned money turning Florian into a frog, you don't know the first thing about me. I move on and I don't look back. Got a date tonight, as a matter of fact."

The sheriff wore an amused expression. "You heard the fairy, Rose. She's innocent. Now, why don't you step out of the closet?" He paused. "Unless you two are comfortable, of course."

Heat burned my cheeks. "Stop blocking the doorway and I'll be happy to leave."

He made a big show of moving aside. "After you." He tipped his hat at Junie. "Thanks for your help, miss."

"No problem." She flashed him a huge smile. "Let me know if you need anything else from me, Sheriff. Anything at all. I love to be of service to my community."

He grinned. "I'll be sure to let you know."

I grabbed his elbow and steered him out of the salon. "Next time, knock before you open a broom closet door."

"And miss the show?" he teased. "I think not."

"There was no show," I insisted. "I was trying to interview her in private."

"You were trying to do something in private."

I gave an exasperated groan. "If you'd been doing your job, you would've already interviewed her."

"I got sidetracked," he said.

"By a shiny penny on the ground?"

His eyes narrowed. "Another frog. This time it was a werewolf."

"Friend of yours?"

"As a matter of fact, yeah. His name's Cayden Mercer. He's a member of the pack."

"Do you allow frogs in the pack?" I queried.

"I have no intention of letting him stay a frog," he said. "As soon as I crack this case, they'll all get turned back to normal."

"I take it Cayden is a playboy," I said.

The sheriff nodded. "Worse than my brother."

Worse than Wyatt? That was saying something.

"Do we have a list of recent dates for Cayden that we can cross-reference with Florian's and Thom's?" I asked.

"Already got it," Sheriff Nash said, pulling a crumpled piece of paper from his back pocket. "There are four names in common. Junie was one of them."

"You believe her story?" I asked.

"Didn't hear all of it. Seems like you did, though," he replied.

"I did."

"I'll accept that."

I cocked an eyebrow. "Why?"

He shrugged. "You seem to have a pretty good minotaur shit detector. I'll move on to the other girls and circle back to Junie if nothing pans out."

"So, who's next?" I asked, reaching for the list.

"No, no." He slid the list into his back pocket. "This is *my* investigation, Rose."

"But I need to cover the story for the paper," I said, trying to retrieve the list from his pocket.

He grabbed my hand before it reached his pocket. "I know it's enticing, but you've got to learn to keep your hands to yourself."

"You don't understand. Aunt Hyacinth specifically requested it."

He stopped moving but continued to hold my hand. "Your aunt asked you to investigate?"

"Not me," I said. "The paper. Bentley is working on it, too."

His expression clouded over. "Can't say I'm surprised."

I cleared my throat and he gave me a quizzical look. I inclined my head toward his hand, still gripping mine.

"Sorry," he said, and let go.

I had to admit, I liked the feel of his hand clutching mine. I quickly brushed the thought aside. Good thing *he* wasn't telepathic.

"Can I please go with you?" I asked. "I promise I'll be more of a help than a hindrance. I don't want to disappoint my aunt. I'm new to the family, and you know what that's like."

"I do," he said darkly. His brother had been an unwelcome addition to the Rose clan when he'd married Linnea. Their subsequent divorce was a blessing in Aunt Hyacinth's eyes, and a relief in Linnea's, although Wyatt seemed to delight in making himself a nuisance.

"So that's a yes?" I asked eagerly.

He exhaled loudly. "Fine. You can come, but let me do the talking."

"Absolutely," I said, but not before crossing my fingers behind my back.

CHAPTER 4

DAKOTA MUSGROVE WAS AS FAR from a showy fairy as you could get. She was a dryad, which, according to Marley, meant she was a tree nymph. When I said she was probably very down-to-earth, Marley clapped her hands over her ears and groaned. Mom jokes never ceased to amuse me.

Dakota worked as a chef in the Lighthouse, one of the nicest restaurants in town. I'd heard all about the revolving top of the lighthouse, which provided a complete view of the town and the adjacent Atlantic Ocean.

"We get to ride to the top?" I asked, as the sheriff and I entered the base of the lighthouse.

"That's where the kitchen is," he said. "You haven't been here yet?"

"No, I haven't eaten out much," I said.

"You don't strike me as a troll," the sheriff said.

"A troll?" I sensed an insult in there somewhere.

"You know, hiding from the world under your bridge."

"Oh. Like a hermit." Okay, not an insult. "Staying home was a financial necessity in New Jersey. We rarely had money for restaurants. Marley and I splurged on diners and Chinese food."

He gave me an understated nod. "I see."

We stepped into the paranormal version of an elevator. It looked like a platform without walls.

"I'm not getting on that death trap," I said. "One strong sneeze and I'll plunge over the side."

He grinned. "Get on, Rose. It's perfectly safe."

"You'd love that, wouldn't you?" I asked. "An easy way to get rid of me."

He chuckled. "Easy? Do you know the mess that would create? Trust me, there are far easier methods."

"Why do I get the idea you've given this some thought?"

He took me by the hand and dragged me onto the platform. He tapped a pedal with his foot and we began to rise. I clutched his arm and pushed myself against him.

"Isn't your daughter supposed to be the anxious one?" he queried.

That much was true. Thanks to her intelligence and the early death of her father, Marley was an anxious child with a fear of many things, including heights. I was generally okay with heights, although this platform was causing me to rethink my opinion.

Sheriff Nash reached out to the side. "Invisible walls, Rose. Go on. Touch it."

Oh. I reached to the side and, sure enough, I felt a wall there. "Why'd you let me think it was empty space?"

He gave me a lopsided grin. "Because it was fun?"

We arrived at the top and the platform delivered us directly into the restaurant. The lunchtime crowd was taking advantage of the gorgeous skyline.

"We probably should've come during the off-hours," I said. "She's going to be busy."

"That's the best reason to come now," the sheriff said. "She'll be too distracted to tell believable lies."

He didn't need to flash his star badge, although it was pretty obvious, stuck to his chest. Everyone we encountered seemed to recognize him with barely a glance.

"Table for two, Sheriff?" an older woman asked, holding two menus. She gave me an appraising look. "She's much prettier than the last one you brought here."

The sheriff's face reddened. "This isn't a date, Alice. We're here on official business."

"Too bad," Alice said. "If you have time, stop for a bite when you're finished. Soup of the day is your favorite."

His brow lifted. "Cracklewhip chowder?"

She nodded.

He sucked in a breath. "I'm sorely tempted, but first I need to talk to Dakota. Is she in the kitchen?"

"She is." Alice looked concerned. "She's very busy right now. Can it wait?"

"Nope. Sorry." The sheriff swaggered across the room and I hustled to keep up.

We found the dryad barking orders in the kitchen. Despite the beads of perspiration on her forehead and her unattractive chef's outfit, she was a natural beauty—no glitter required. With her rich brown hair and flawless skin, it wasn't hard to see the attraction.

"Sheriff, the kitchen is insanely busy right now," Dakota said, scrutinizing a dish in front of her. "Who's responsible for this? It looks like mermaid vomit."

"We need a word, Dakota," the sheriff said. "The kitchen won't fall apart in two minutes."

"Says a man who microwaves his meals." She wiped her brow with a cloth and maneuvered through the kitchen toward us. "Let's go into my office, where it's quiet."

We followed her to a small room off the kitchen, and she closed the door behind us.

"What's up?" she asked.

"Need to ask you about some of your recent dates," he said.

She squinted. "Recent dates? Why?"

"It's my understanding that you've been out with Florian Rose-Muldoon, Thom Rutledge, and Cayden Mercer."

She crossed her arms and glared at us. "What's it to you?" Her deep scowl had no impact on her beautiful features.

"Would it surprise you to learn that they're currently living their lives as frogs?" Sheriff Nash asked.

It seemed to take a moment for the news to sink in. Dakota struggled to find the right words.

"I'm sorry. Did you just say they're *frogs*?"

"That's right," the sheriff said.

She burst into throaty laughter. "That's brilliant. Who did that?"

The sheriff stared at her, waiting for the realization to take hold. Her almond-shaped eyes widened.

"Me? Are you serious? I'm a dryad. We don't do transformation spells."

"But it would be simple enough to pay someone to perform a few spells," the sheriff said. "Maybe a chance for revenge?"

"Revenge for what?" Dakota asked. "I dumped all three of their sorry butts. One date each was more than they deserved."

I warmed to her immediately. "Preach, sister."

She gave me the once-over. "Is she a new deputy or something? What happened to the leprechaun? Did his luck finally run out?"

"Deputy Bolan is still my right arm," the sheriff said.

"I'm not law enforcement," I said. "I work for *Vox Populi*." The statement still felt foreign on my tongue.

"She's chasing the same leads I am," the sheriff said.

"And you let her come with you?" Dakota studied me. "I guess I can see why."

I shot the sheriff a quizzical look, but his expression remained blank.

"Why'd you give them the heave ho?" the sheriff asked.

Dakota looked thoughtful. "Well, Thom just wanted to feed off me. I feed people for a living. I didn't need that at home, as well."

Perfectly understandable.

"Cayden couldn't keep his gaze pinned on me for more than sixty seconds before his head was turned by some busty blonde. I left that date midway through. I'm far too busy to waste my time on that minotaur shit."

"And Florian?" I prompted.

She hesitated. "To be honest, I actually liked Florian."

"Then why only one date?" I asked.

"Because I know his reputation," she said. "If he'd managed another date, he would have charmed me into sleeping with him, and then that would have been the end of it."

"How do you know you wouldn't have been different?" I asked.

She gave me a regretful smile. "Because I'm not a witch. Everyone with half a brain knows that his mother won't allow him to marry outside the coven."

"Then why go out with him at all?" I asked.

Her arms dropped to her sides. "Have you *seen* Florian? How could I resist?"

She had a point. Cousin or not, even I recognized the white-blond hunk of beauty that was Florian Rose-Muldoon.

"Can you think of anyone who would've held a grudge

against these three guys?" I asked. "You had conversations with all of them. Maybe a common name popped up."

Her expression brightened. "It's not a grudge, but they all get their hair cut at the same barbershop. Maybe the barber's heard something."

"Which one?" the sheriff asked.

"Snips-n-Clips," she said. "I remember being surprised. I expected Florian to go somewhere more upscale."

"Thanks for the tip," Sheriff Nash said.

"Stay for lunch, won't you?" Dakota asked. "My treat."

Sheriff Nash glanced at me. "How about it, Rose? You hungry?"

"Really?" I figured the last thing he'd want to do was share a meal with me.

He placed a hand over his sheriff's star. "I consider it my civic duty to make sure you've tried cracklewhip chowder."

I shrugged. "I'll try anything once," I said.

He flashed a lopsided grin. "I'll bear that in mind, Rose."

"What's so special about cracklewhip chowder?" I asked.

We were seated at a small table next to the floor-to-ceiling window. I watched the scenery go by as we slowly rotated at the top of the lighthouse—the sparkling blue water of the Atlantic, the mysterious Fairy Cove, Mariner's Landing, and then around to the picturesque town on the other side. A perfect viewpoint.

"You have to taste it to understand," he said, and held out his spoon. "You're welcome to try some."

I wrinkled my nose.

He peered at me. "You're one of those, aren't you?"

I straightened in my chair. "One of what?"

"The kind of person that doesn't share food off the same

fork. I bet no one is allowed to sip out of your coffee cup, either. You probably put a protection spell on it."

I tried to hide my guilty expression. "I don't know what you mean. I don't even know how to do a protection spell." Yet.

He held the spoon closer to my mouth. "So taste it, then."

"I don't want to."

He grinned and popped the spoon into his mouth. "Use your own spoon, then." He pushed the bowl across the table toward me.

"It does look good," I said, lifting my spoon and digging in. It felt oddly intimate, eating chowder out of the sheriff's bowl. I wasn't up on werewolf culture, but I figured they weren't shy about sharing meals, so this was no big deal.

The sheriff watched me eat with a combination of amusement and satisfaction. "Amazing, right?"

I nodded, my mouth full of chowder. It tasted salty and flavorful, like ingesting the sea but not in the horrible way that gets water up your nose.

"Do you like your scallops?" he asked, and pulled the bowl back toward him.

"Love 'em." I bit into another one and sighed with pleasure. They weren't magical, but they were magically delicious.

"Gonna offer me any?" the sheriff asked.

"If you promise to use your own fork."

His grin widened as he speared one. "Tell me about New Jersey."

"What do you want to know?"

"Is it as crowded as everyone says?" he asked, slurping more soup off his spoon. Normally, I wasn't a fan of slurping, but something about the way Sheriff Nash did it made it seem charming, almost sexy.

"Depends on where you are," I said. "There are plenty of

parts of the state that are rural. You just need to know where to go."

"Did you live in a rural area?" More slurping.

I shook my head. "I wasn't far from Philadelphia."

"But that's in Pennsylvania."

"Yes. Right across the Delaware River."

"Huh," he said, and scraped the last of his soup from the bottom of the bowl. "What did you think of Dakota?"

"Besides the fact that she's insanely beautiful?" I queried.

"I don't think her appearance tells us whether she's guilty."

"That's very sensible of you, Sheriff."

He winked. "I try my best."

"I don't think she's responsible," I said. "She's too straightforward. She doesn't seem like someone who would resort to magic. If she likes you enough, she'll give you another chance. If not, you're out."

"Sounds like that's probably your approach, too. You could come back another time, compare notes with her on your dating experience."

I laughed. "Dating experience?"

"Sure," he said. "Attractive woman like you. I imagine you have experience."

"Hardly. I married my husband when we were still children ourselves. We had Marley immediately, so dating was never really an option."

He fell silent for a moment. "When did he die?"

"Four years ago. An accident on the road. He was a truck driver."

"And you haven't dated since?"

"No." I leaned back in my chair. "Didn't I tell you all this already?"

"You told me you qualified as a…born-again Maiden, was it?" he said. "But that doesn't mean you didn't date."

I splayed my hands on the table. "I didn't date."

"Okay, then. Glad we established that."

"Why?" I asked.

He blinked. "Why what?"

"Why are you glad we established that?"

He looked confused. "Just trying to get a handle on your history, Rose. Never a bad thing for the sheriff to get to know new citizens, especially from the human world."

"You know you called me attractive, right?"

The sheriff rolled his eyes. "I think even Deputy Bolan would agree with that statement, and he thinks you're a pain in his green rear. It's not exactly breaking news."

"Maybe it is to me."

"Then you should probably alert the media. Tell your boss so he can print it in the next paper."

We stared at each other for a beat too long, until the vibration of my phone made me jump.

"Hot date?" the sheriff asked. "Oh, wait. Of course not. You don't date."

I looked at the phone. "It's a reminder from Aster. She's picking me up in an hour to head over to the tourism board office." And I'd nearly forgotten all about it. Some Rose I was.

He inclined his head. "You're working there, too?"

"Volunteering," I said. "My family seems big on community service."

"Community meddling is more like it," he grumbled.

"Thanks for suggesting we stay and eat," I said. "It was the best meal I've had in Starry Hollow so far."

He opened his mouth to say something, but then seemed to think better of it. "No worries, Rose. Why don't I drive you home?"

The Starry Hollow Tourism Board was located on Enchanted

Road not far from the library. Aster insisted on driving me in her car, even though Aunt Hyacinth had offered her driver.

"Her driver isn't magical," I said. "Why don't you accept the offer?" Aster had told me before that she and her husband tried to use as little magic as possible in the house, so that their four-year-old twins wouldn't become too dependent once they came into their magic at age eleven.

"It isn't about magic," Aster said. "As much as I don't want to be reliant on magic, I also don't want to be reliant on Mother."

She parked the car and we walked up to the Colonial-style brick building with its inviting white front porch and cherry red door. Flowers bloomed from hanging pots and a flag of Starry Hollow swayed proudly in the breeze. A black lantern burned above the entryway.

"That's not a light bulb," I said, observing the lantern.

"No, some businesses and residences prefer fey lanterns," she said. "You'll find a mixture of that in town. Some people cling to their magic in any and every possible way."

"Well, I guess it makes sense for the tourism board to show off their magic." Flaunt it if you've got it.

"But we cater to paranormals," Aster said. "Personally, I don't see the need to advertise the magical elements. Starry Hollow has plenty to offer that isn't magical."

I disagreed, but that was probably because the whole idea of a magical town was still new to me.

We entered the building where a man greeted us...Okay, not a man. He had a man's upper half but a horse's lower half. A horse man? No, wait. A centaur. I silently thanked Marley for her impressive mythological knowledge.

"Good afternoon, Thaddeus," Aster said. "I'd like you to meet my cousin, Ember Rose."

"Of course. I heard all about your dramatic arrival. Most exciting news." Thaddeus smiled at me and trotted over to shake my hand. "Thaddeus Taylor at your service, Miss Rose."

"Ember is going to be working with us as a volunteer," Aster said, her fingers gliding absently across her pearl necklace.

"Splendid," Thaddeus said. "We can always use another pair of hands."

I glanced around the bright and airy space. The interior was as charming as the exterior, with wooden floorboards and rustic furniture. The room was filled with books, brochures, framed photographs, and trinkets that represented all the good things in Starry Hollow. I noticed a replica of the Lighthouse and my expression brightened.

"I had lunch in the restaurant earlier today," I said, touching the top of the lighthouse. "It was amazing. I would go back for the views, even if the food was terrible." Which, thankfully, it wasn't.

Aster gazed at me with interest. "Did you dine on your own? You should have called me. I'm always up for lunch, unless I'm volunteering or with the boys."

"I wasn't alone," I said. "I was with Sheriff Nash."

I heard a slight choking sound from Aster. "I'm sorry. Did you just say you had lunch with Granger Nash?"

"We were talking to Dakota, the chef there," I said.

"I see," Aster said. "She had a date with Florian recently, didn't she?"

I nodded. "As well as with the other two frogs."

"Do you think she did it?" Thaddeus asked, intrigued. "I don't mean to pry, but people can talk of little else right now."

"Definitely not," I said. "She actually liked Florian, for one thing."

"Somebody has to," Aster muttered.

"Are you working for the sheriff?" Thaddeus asked. "Did something happen to Deputy Bolan?"

I gave a dismissive wave. "No, I'm working on a story for *Vox Populi*. The sheriff agreed to let me shadow him as a favor to my aunt." Okay, that last part was a lie, but it seemed better than 'the sheriff thinks I am annoying and wants to make sure I don't damage his case.'

"I see we have the new brochures out," Aster said. She plucked a colorful pamphlet from a display case and paged through it.

I peered over her shoulder. "I don't see the broomstick tour on there. That was incredible. You get such a great view of the town. Marley wants to do it again." And Marley was deathly afraid of heights, so that was high praise, indeed— pun intended.

Thaddeus offered a sheepish grin. "Aster feels that we should highlight other aspects of Starry Hollow."

"Absolutely," Aster said. "Witches from around the country can ride broomsticks. They don't need to join a tour."

I hesitated. "I see your point, but not everybody in our tour group was a witch or wizard. Because the broomsticks are operated by magic, all sorts of paranormals took advantage of it."

I looked through the rest of the brochure. It seemed like a brochure from any beach town in America. It emphasized the location, the wide, sandy beaches, and the pristine water. At least it included a list of shops and a directory.

"What's the Wish Market?" I hadn't noticed that in my travels through town.

"Nothing special," Aster said. "Every paranormal town has one. That's why it's only listed in the directory."

Thaddeus cleared his throat. "Perhaps your cousin would

like a little more information, considering she has no experience with Wish Markets in the human world."

I looked at Aster expectantly.

"Of course," she said. "How silly of me. I'll do better than explain it. How about I take you there?"

"I don't have time today," I said. "But I'd love to go another time." Whatever the Wish Market was, it sounded pretty cool.

"Absolutely," Aster said. "We'll make the arrangements."

"So, what do you promote as the big selling point of the town?" I asked.

"You're looking at it," Aster said, tapping the brochure. "Sun, sea, and shops."

"What's your slogan?" I asked.

"Slogan for what?" Aster queried.

"The town," I replied. "How do you grab the attention of potential tourists?"

Aster shook the brochure at me. "I told you already."

"Okay, in the human world, lots of tourist destinations have slogans. Virginia is for Lovers. What Happens in Vegas Stays in Vegas. Disney World uses the Happiest Place on Earth or Where Dreams Come True."

Thaddeus puffed out a breath of air. "Dreams coming true in the human world? Most unlikely."

"What about other paranormal tourist traps?" I asked. "What do they emphasize about their towns?"

"Well, there's Mistfall," Aster said. "They emphasize their unique atmosphere."

"I have no frame of reference," I said, "but I assume not all paranormal towns are like this one."

"Obviously not," Aster snapped. "That's why we have a healthy stream of tourists. For the beaches."

"And excellent dining," Thaddeus added.

I found it hard to believe that was all Starry Hollow had

to offer other paranormals. I was going to need to get to know the town better so that I could offer suggestions. Coming from the human world, of course, everything about Starry Hollow seemed interesting and amazing.

"Did the new china arrive?" Aster asked.

"The box is in your office," Thaddeus replied.

"Excellent," she said, and her heels clipped across the wooden floor to a private office in the back room.

"You have an office here?" I asked.

"Of course," she said. "I have an office anywhere I serve on the board."

She snapped her fingers and the box popped open. Plates floated out in a neatly stacked pile and landed gently on the desk.

"What are those for?" I asked.

"Collectors," Aster replied. She held one up for my inspection. On the plate was a hand-painted image of Palmetto House, Linnea's inn, with 'Starry Hollow' written in gold script underneath.

"That's pretty," I said.

"Tourists love the architecture here," she said. "I try to include a variety of popular buildings. The Whitethorn was last year's plate."

"What's the Whitethorn?" I asked.

Her eyes rounded. "You haven't been there yet?"

I shook my head. "Another restaurant?"

"A pub down past Fairy Cove and the Lighthouse. It's one of the oldest establishments in town. You can feel ancient magic at work in there."

I shivered at the mention of ancient magic. "What do you mean?"

She inhaled deeply. "You'll have to experience it for your-self. There are lots of stories associated with the Whitethorn. Vampire pirates, hidden gold. It's fascinating."

"Vampire pirates?" I echoed. "I'm sorry. Can you repeat that?"

"Captain Blackfang and his band of merry marauders," Aster said.

"How could there be pirates on the high seas?" I asked. "Isn't it the magic of the paranormal towns that protects them from the sun?"

"It's part of the legend," Aster said. "Their ships were enchanted. You absolutely must go to the Whitethorn."

"The only pub I've been to is the Wishing Well," I said.

Aster tried to disguise her dismay. "I know it's convenient to the cottage, but it really doesn't attract the right sort of clientele."

"The sheriff isn't the right sort of clientele?"

"I don't mean Granger specifically," she said. "It just tends to be where shifters and other non-users of magic congregate."

I bit back a smile. "You sound like your mother."

"Thank you," Aster said.

"Well, I enjoyed the Wishing Well, so I'll probably go again, but I'd love to check out the Whitethorn. It sounds awesome."

"Maybe Sterling and I can hire a babysitter and take you one evening."

I pondered the offer. The thought of uptight Aster and her equally uptight husband hanging out with me in a vampire pirate pub wasn't very appealing.

"Thanks. I'll let you know," I said.

"I suppose you don't have any leads on Florian," she said. "I know Mother is concerned. She had three juniper juleps at lunch today."

"Oh, is that a lot more than usual?"

Aster cocked her head. "More? No, it's far fewer. I'm worried about her mental health."

"That's...understandable." I coughed. "Well, Dakota gave us a lead, so she wasn't a complete dead end. Apparently, all three frogs get their hair cut at the same place. Maybe someone there knows something."

She groaned. "I don't know why Florian insists on going to that dreadful shop when there are plenty of appropriate salons in town."

"Probably because he knows it bugs you." What else were brothers for?

Aster tucked a strand of white-blond hair behind her ear. "You're absolutely right, Ember. Whenever he thinks we're pushing him, his instinct is to resist."

"Because he's a Rose?"

She snorted. "Certainly not. It's because he's a child trapped in a man's body. We need to free the child, so the man has a chance to live his life to the fullest and stop wasting it."

"I think you're overlooking one key fact," I said.

"What's that?"

"We need to free them both from the frog's body first."

Aster sighed. "Yes, Ember. We certainly do."

CHAPTER 5

I WAS SURPRISED to see the sheriff's car pull up in front of the cottage the next morning. Now what? Was he here to warn me against interfering in his investigation again? I thought we'd reached a truce at the Lighthouse, but maybe not.

I didn't wait for him to come to the door. Instead, I met him at the wrought iron gate.

"Good morning, Rose," he greeted me. "Your flowers are looking a little rough around the edges." He nodded toward one of the rose bushes.

I glanced at the flowers wrapped around the fence. "Am I supposed to do something for them? I assume Aunt Hyacinth uses a gardener." Because I certainly had no skills in the floral department. Someone had brought me an orchid recently and I put Marley in charge of it so that I didn't kill it.

"I'm sure she does," the sheriff said. "For a powerful witch, your aunt doesn't do much for herself."

"What brings you here, Sheriff?" I asked. "Are you going to arrest me for chewing too loudly at lunch yesterday?"

He cocked his head, pretending to think. "That loud

sound was you? And here I was blaming termites in the woodwork."

"Hardy har," I said. "I hear the Pot of Gold is looking for a new act. If you're in the market for a second job, you should swing by."

He eyed me curiously. "Been to the Pot of Gold already, have you?"

In truth, I hadn't been to the comedy club, but I'd heard mention of it during a meeting of the Council of Elders. The club was owned by Mervin O'Malley, a leprechaun on the council.

"I'm not here to give you a hard time," the sheriff said. "As much fun as that is. I'm heading over to Snips-n-Clips and thought I'd see if you wanted a ride."

I gave him a suspicious look. "Why? I thought you wanted me to stay out of your investigation."

He shrugged. "Same reason I let you come to the Lighthouse. Dakota mentioned it to both of us, so I figure you'd be turning up there anyway. I may as well do the guy a public service and save him from answering the same questions twice."

"And it enables you to keep an eye on me," I said. "Make sure I don't cause any trouble."

He wagged a finger at me. "Smart and pretty. Rose, you're turning all the stereotypes on their heads."

"Flattery will get you everywhere," I said. "Let me just grab my handbag."

As I turned back toward the cottage, I heard a low growl coming from behind the rosebush. I stopped and peeked around the corner. Prescott Peabody III was in a crouched position, his tail stiff. I scooped him up in my arms.

"What's the matter with you? I'm only going out for a little while. I'll be back in plenty of time for your dinner. For crying out loud, you've just had breakfast."

The sheriff appeared behind me. "It's not that. It's me. He smells the wolf."

I looked back at PP3. "Is that true, buddy? Does this guy stink?" The Yorkie licked the tip of my nose in response. "You don't have to be territorial. He's not moving in on your turf."

I glanced at the sheriff over my shoulder. "Tell him you're not a threat."

The sheriff chuckled. "Why? You think he'll believe me?"

"Why wouldn't he?"

The sheriff hesitated. "Okay, fine. Listen up, little fella. I'm making no claim on your territory. You can pee anywhere you like." Sheriff Nash glanced at me. "Will that do?"

PP3's growl subsided. I carried him back into the cottage, retrieved my handbag, and closed the door.

"Your chariot awaits, miss," the sheriff said, opening the passenger side door.

"At least you don't want me to ride in the back," I said.

"Not today," he said. "But it wouldn't surprise me in the least if that day comes."

I slid in beside him and gave him a look of mock indignation. "What are you suggesting? I'm harboring latent criminal tendencies that will emerge in time?"

He started the car and pulled away from the cottage. "Maybe not criminal tendencies, but definitely trouble-making tendencies. I have a sixth sense about these things."

"Is that a wolf thing?"

He kept his gaze fixed on the road. "Nope. That's a sheriff thing."

Snips-n-Clips was located on Juniper Street, two blocks off Coastline Drive. From the outside, it looked like a traditional barbershop. It even had the rotating red and white pole out front. The interior, however, was another matter.

The moment we stepped through the door, I noticed floating razors and a bar set up in the corner of the room. A couple of customers were enjoying a glass of ale in their chairs, while a magical razor worked its way around their heads.

"Beer at this hour?" I queried.

The sheriff seemed unconcerned. "Breakfast of champions. Anyway, it's probably a breakfast ale."

I cast a sidelong glance at him. "Breakfast ale? Is that a real thing?"

"It is here. It's chock-full of magical properties. Like stopping for a coffee with a shot of confidence."

The receptionist spotted us standing in front of the door and gestured us over to the front desk.

"Good morning, Sheriff Nash," the woman said. "Are you here for a haircut?"

"Not today," he said. "I'm looking for Ben. Is he around?"

"He sure is," she said. "He ran into the back a minute ago to retrieve a bottle of bucksberry fizz for one of the customers. He requested something more festive than ale."

"Talk about VIP service," I said. No wonder Florian came here. It seemed that each customer was treated like royalty. I wasn't sure how comfortable I'd be with magical razors near my throat, though. Seemed too risky to have them unmanned. I wondered how much his business insurance ran him.

A slight man emerged from the back with a champagne-shaped bottle and sporting the telltale ears of an elf. He stopped short when he saw the sheriff.

"Excellent. Have you finally decided to try somewhere other than your mother's kitchen?" Ben asked.

Sheriff Nash broke into a broad smile. "Don't go revealing all my secrets, Ben."

"Sorry about that, but anyone with half an eye can see that it isn't a professional cut." He placed the bottle on the bar and proceeded to pop the cork. "If you just let me take care of this customer's drink, I'll be with you in a moment."

"There's no rush," the sheriff said.

I knew what the sheriff was thinking. That gave us the opportunity to look around and scope out the employees and the clientele in case there was a clue. The only woman present was the receptionist and she seemed far too old and plain to attract the attention of the three bachelors in question. Of course, maybe that was the problem. Maybe they'd spurned her and she'd taken her revenge.

"So how long have you been working here?" I asked her.

"Since Ben opened the shop five years ago," she said. "I helped him establish the magic in here. That's why I own a quarter of the business."

My brow lifted. And here I thought she was just the receptionist. My radar was clearly switched in the off position this morning.

"How did you help him establish the magic?" Maybe she was a witch.

"Technically, it was a fairy friend of hers," Ben interjected. "But Robina oversaw everything. She was basically the project manager."

"I'm actually a fairy, too," the receptionist said, and noticed my confused expression. "I know what you're thinking. I've got no wings."

The sheriff took a renewed interest in the receptionist. "You served time?"

I jerked my head toward the sheriff. Served time?

"Yes, Sheriff," she said. "The name's Robina Mapperton. I hail from Blue Moon Valley."

"That's another paranormal town," the sheriff said, for my benefit. "We should have a record of your relocation to Starry Hollow in my office."

"That's right," Robina said. "I had to turn in my passport

when I arrived. If I ever want to leave here, I need to apply for it to be returned."

He nodded. "Thanks for your disclosure."

"How do you know Ben?" Robina asked the sheriff.

"We played basketball together on an intramural team last year," the sheriff said.

"Nearly won the championship, too." Ben approached us with a flute in each hand. "Since the bottle's open, can I offer you a light refreshment?"

"Not while I'm on duty, but thanks," the sheriff said.

"I don't know what it is," I said. "I wouldn't mind trying one, though." I plucked the flute from his hand and took a sip. It was fizzy and sweet.

"The customer that requested the bottle is celebrating," Ben said. "He's getting married tomorrow."

"Lucky him," I said.

"Or unlucky him," the sheriff said, "depending."

Ben laughed. "Sheriff Nash, that's awfully cynical of you. I happen to think marriage is the best decision a man can make in his life."

"I'm sure your wife would be happy to hear you say that," I said.

"Oh, Ben's not married," Robina said, with a regretful sigh. "Not for my lack of trying."

Ben blushed, turning the ends of his pointy ears a bright pink. He was attractive in that elfin sort of way. Cute, rather than undeniably hot like Sheriff Nash.

"Is there somewhere we can talk for a minute?" the sheriff asked.

"Of course," Ben said. "My office is just this way." He turned back to Robina. "You'll hold down the fort, won't you? Make sure nobody nicks an artery."

She smiled. "You know you can count on me."

We followed Ben into a bright and sunny office adjacent

to the main room. He perched on the edge of his desk and gestured for us to have a seat.

I dropped into one of the chairs, still sipping my bucksberry fizz. The more I drank, the more delicious it tasted.

"So, what brings you here?" Ben asked. "Robina hasn't violated her parole, has she?"

The sheriff shook his head. "I'm not here about Robina."

"Why is she missing her wings?" I interjected. I'd been dying to ask since the moment she mentioned it.

"Sometimes fairies have their wings clipped as punishment for their crimes," the sheriff explained. "In some cases, they simply bind the wings together, but in more serious cases, the wings are removed."

My eyes grew round. "How serious?"

"It doesn't matter," Ben said. "Robina has been with me for five years and she's never been anything other than honest and hard working. This place couldn't have been successful without her help."

"You'll have to forgive Miss Rose," the sheriff said. "She didn't mean to be rude. She's new to town and doesn't know a lot about the paranormal world."

Ben's expression brightened and he fixed his attention on me. "You're the missing Rose girl. How exciting. Your cousin Florian is a customer here."

"I know," I said. "That's why we're here, in fact."

Ben frowned. "Is there a problem? I would think if he was unhappy with the service, it wouldn't require the sheriff's involvement."

"I'm not sure if you've heard the news," Sheriff Nash said, "but Florian Rose-Muldoon is currently living life as a small green frog."

Ben started to laugh, but then thought better of it. "How in Nature's name did that happen? A spell gone awry?"

The sheriff shrugged. "That's what we're trying to figure

out. He's not the only one, either. Thom Rutledge and Cayden Mercer have also been turned into frogs by an unseen hand."

Ben stroked his chin. "Well, I can see why you've come to me. All three of them are clients here."

"We went to see Dakota at the Lighthouse yesterday," the sheriff said. "She had recent interactions with all three gentlemen and mentioned that they each came here for haircuts. We were hoping that you might have overheard something helpful."

Ben sighed. "Dakota Musgrove. She's something else, isn't she? Smart, successful, beautiful."

"Those were my thoughts, too," I said.

Sheriff Nash shot me a quizzical look. "Were they now?"

"Settle down, Sheriff," I said. "I can appreciate the good qualities of another woman without it making me a lesbian. Not that there's anything wrong with that."

"Have you noticed any issues with these particular clients?" the sheriff asked, returning his focus to Ben. "Did they have any problems with other customers while they were here? Any interactions with Robina that you noticed?"

Ben considered the question for a moment. "No disagreements that I recall. They're always in here in good cheer, regaling us with stories of their exploits." He cringed and glanced at me. "Apologies. I mean, relationships."

"You don't need to sugarcoat anything for me," I said. "I had a strip club at the end of my block. I saw plenty of exploits."

"She's from New Jersey," the sheriff added helpfully.

"There is one name that comes to mind," Ben said, still thinking. "I'm pretty sure I've heard at least two of them mention Artemis Haverford."

The sheriff leaned forward slightly. "Two of them were involved with the matchmaker?"

Ben shrugged. "I can't say for sure."

"Why would they need a matchmaker?" I asked.

"Because they're eligible bachelors in search of companionship," Ben said.

"But it sounds to me like they don't have any trouble attracting companions," I said. "Why would they feel the need to visit a matchmaker?"

"Artemis Haverford isn't your typical matchmaker," the sheriff said. "She offers a bit more than you think."

"You mean she's a madam?" And here I thought Starry Hollow was a sweet little magical town. Maybe there was a seedy underbelly, after all.

The sheriff gave an embarrassed chuckle. "No, no. That's not what I mean at all. We may have our problems here in town, but prostitution isn't one of them. Thank Mother Nature."

Well, that was a relief. I didn't like the idea of Florian going to visit a magical madam.

"Thanks for your help, Ben," the sheriff said. "We appreciate it."

"Robina isn't in any trouble, is she?" he asked, a note of concern in his voice.

"I'll need to do a routine check on her documentation," the sheriff said, "but it sounds to me like everything's in order."

Ben looked relieved. "She's been more than a business partner to me, you see. Robina's like a mother figure. My own mother died when I was young, so it's been nice to have an older woman to look after me the way she does."

I sympathized. "It was nice to meet you, Ben."

He gave me a shy smile. "You, too. If you're interested in having someone show you around town, I'd be happy to oblige."

His offer took me by surprise. "Um, sure. I work at *Vox*

Populi. You can reach me there most days." I wasn't ready to hand out my cell phone number to every elf with a bottle of bucksberry fizz, no matter how delicious it tasted.

Ben nodded happily. "Okay, I look forward to it."

Sheriff Nash had the decency to wait until we left the building to start his relentless mockery. "Picking up new admirers wherever you go, huh, Rose?"

"I would think you'd be insulted," I said airily.

"Insulted? Why?"

"Why didn't he assume that we have a thing going on? He asked me out right under your nose." I whistled. "That's ballsy."

The sheriff scratched his cheek. "I hadn't really thought about it like that. I guess he could just tell there was nothing between us."

Now it was my turn to feel insulted. "I guess so."

He turned on the radio and we drove back to the cottage in relative silence.

CHAPTER 6

I KNOCKED on the door of Palmetto House, but there was no answer. I'd decided to drop in and see whether Linnea knew any of Florian's secrets that might help identify the culprit. Between Aster and Linnea, I was sure that Florian was more likely to confide in the eldest sibling. I knew that would be my choice.

I clicked open the door and walked through the beautifully styled living room to the back staircase that led to Linnea's personal quarters.

I found my cousin in her bedroom, buried under a mountain of laundry. Her white-blond hair was pulled back in a ponytail and she wore a lilac-colored tracksuit. Very unRoselike.

"Ember, is that you?" a muffled voice said.

"Yes." I moved aside a few piles of clothes to reach her. "Why don't you use magic to deal with this?"

"I'm depleted," she said, stretching out on the bed in the middle of folded towels. "I had to clean the kitchen and the bathrooms today."

"If magic takes that much out of you, why not hire cleaners?" I asked. "I've seen ads for fairy cleaners all over town."

Linnea looked at me like I had two heads. "No self-respecting witch would ever have a fairy cleaning service. That's like admitting that you aren't good at magic."

"But you're an amazing witch," I said. "I've seen your kickass powers." She'd tossed Jimmy the Lighter across my apartment with the flick of her wrist. She belonged in black leather with thigh-high boots, not in a lilac tracksuit.

"That was different," Linnea said. "You were in danger. Adrenaline kicked in."

"Like when I made it rain," I said.

"Exactly. Survival taps into our deepest magical reserves." She glanced helplessly around the bed at the piles of laundry. "Although I often feel like I'm hanging on by a thread. Being a single mother is hard, with or without magic."

"Preach it, sister...er, cousin." I picked up a stack of towels. "I'll help you. Where do these go?"

"Ember, you don't need to do that," she said. "You have your own busy schedule to worry about."

"I owe you for saving my life," I said.

She blew a raspberry. "You owe me nothing."

"What about your kids?" I asked. "They're old enough to be doing more around the inn."

"They help when they can," she said. "It's more important to me that they focus on school and their extracurricular activities. I want them to attend a good university, so they have as many choices in life as possible."

"Paranormal universities?" It hadn't occurred to me that they had their own higher education system.

"Of course." She lifted a pile of clothes and began putting socks in the top drawer of her dresser. "Bryn really wants to attend Angel Oak University. It's close enough to come home when she wants to, but not so close that I could drop in unexpectedly."

"She's only fourteen," I said. "You have a few years to go."

"They go by so quickly, though," Linnea said, her arms now empty. "And Bryn is all about preparation. She basically raises herself."

I smiled. "She sounds like Marley."

Linnea picked up another pile of laundry. "They are very similar. They remind me of Aster."

I balked. "Aster?"

"Miss Perfect? Yes, of course." Linnea inclined her head. "You don't think so?"

"I really don't know Aster well enough to say, but she seems so…" I groped for the right word. "Stiff and repressed." Until she's kicked back a few cocktails, that is.

"She's also very organized and together," Linnea said. She smiled at me over top of the laundry pile. "Unlike me."

"She has Sterling to help and she isn't running a busy inn," I said. I empathized with Linnea's struggles.

"That's because she made better choices," Linnea said. "She didn't fall in love with a wereass."

"Don't be so hard on yourself," I said. I scooped up a set of folded sheets. "Tell me where these go."

She sighed. "The linen closet. This way."

We placed our piles in the linen closet and an idea occurred to me. "You know, I'll need to practice my magic sooner or later. Why don't you help me and, that way, I can help you?"

"Practice how?"

I shrugged. "I don't know. Teach me a few spells that I can do around the house. That helps me, too. I can use them in the cottage." I smiled. "Trust me, Marley will thank you."

Linnea chewed her lip. "I don't know. Mother wants your training done in a certain way. She's very particular."

I placed a hand on my hip. "Linnea, you need help and I want to learn magic. It's a win-win."

She appeared thoughtful for a moment. "Okay, but you have to promise not to tell Mother. She'd have my head on one of her silver platters."

"She won't while Florian is still a frog," I said. "She won't risk losing two children."

Linnea heaved a sigh. "Poor Florian. The kids keep asking about him. They're worried they're going to have an amphibian for an uncle forever."

"Hopefully not. There are multiple people working on the case, including me."

"Aster thinks Florian probably got what he deserved. That he finally stepped on the toes of the wrong woman."

"I try not to say what anyone else deserves," I said. "It's hard to know the real reason for someone's behavior."

"True. I'm sure the whole town thought I was insane to marry Wyatt." She snorted. "Guess I should have listened to the naysayers."

"I was hoping you might have insight into Florian's recent dating life. Anyone you can think of that might not be on Simon's list?"

"I wish I had a clue," Linnea said. "He and I haven't talked that much lately. I'm always so busy."

"Maybe Florian can help you," I suggested.

Linnea burst into laughter. "Not likely. Florian is a spoiled wizard that doesn't want to grow up and be responsible."

"That sounds like what Aster would say. Is that what you really think?"

Linnea walked back to the bedroom and I followed. "Not really. I've just heard it bandied about so often, I've adopted the same attitude."

"It sounds to me like he's constantly under your mother's thumb and struggling to get out from under," I said.

Linnea nodded. "We all are, except Aster, because she does everything right."

"She's struggling, too. Trust me. What about the first time she doesn't?" I asked. "Aster is probably scared to death at what might happen, so she colors inside the lines."

"Mother raised us with an iron wand," Linnea agreed. "It definitely leaves an impression." She brightened. "Speaking of which, I'll get my beginner's wand out for you."

She went to the bedroom closet and pulled a box from the shelf, retrieving a bright red case.

"That looks like a giant lipstick tube," I said.

She laughed. "I had gaudy taste back then. Mother was horrified that I came home with this one as my first wand."

"Your first act of rebellion," I said.

Linnea smiled and gazed at the case. "I guess it was." She popped it open and handed me the wand. "I'd hoped to give it to one of my kids one day, but you know how that turned out."

I nodded. "Werewolves." When a witch or wizard had children with a werewolf, the child could end up as one or the other, but not both. Linnea ended up with two werewolves, much to her mother's disappointment.

"The wand helps you focus," she said. "Hopefully, it won't be necessary as you develop your magical skills."

"Because I'm a Rose?"

She winked. "Especially because you're a Rose."

I paused, uncertain whether to ask my next question. "Do you believe all the hoopla about the One True Witch?"

Linnea looked taken aback. "Of course. Why wouldn't I?"

"I don't know. It sounds so…elitist."

"Maybe it is, but that doesn't make it untrue."

"Will I learn about the OTW in any of my training?"

I asked.

"I'm sure Mother would be happy to arrange it. She wants you to know everything about your heritage."

"I'd rather know everything about my family. I'd love to see pictures of my parents. Do you know if your mother has any?"

"I'm sure she must," Linnea said. "You'll need to ask when she's in the right mood, though."

"Ha. How can you tell when that is?"

"Years of practice."

We laughed.

"I need to restock the towels in the guest bedrooms upstairs," Linnea said. "Why don't we start there?"

We each carried a laundry basket up two flights of stairs to the inn bedrooms. My thigh muscles burned by the time we reached the top.

"That's a good workout," I said. "You know, I've been meaning to ask—what do you pay in property taxes on a place like this?" Real estate websites didn't include paranormal towns, so I couldn't snoop like I used to do in the human world.

"It's not too onerous," Linnea said. "Even Mother's taxes are reasonable, given the size of Thornhold."

I set down my laundry basket and pulled the wand from my waistband. "Now what?"

"You focus your will on the wand," Linnea said. "Then you do a spell on the towels. The easiest one would be a spell that sends all the towels to their respective places at once. You expend less energy that way."

"What about telekinesis?" I asked. "Will that use up more of my energy than a spell?"

"Depends." Linnea examined me. "What did you manage to do in your assessment?"

"I moved a feather."

"A feather," Linnea repeated, unimpressed.

"And I saw cards in my head," I added quickly, not wanting to be seen as a loser. "Marigold thinks I have potential."

"Let's stick with a spell for now," Linnea said. "I don't want to interfere with Marigold's training."

She told me how to grip the wand without getting a cramp in my hand and aim it without seeming like I was threatening the towels.

"Are the towels capable of feeling threatened?" I queried.

"Not in the way that you or I would, but there's a definite energy to this. You don't want to intimidate the towels with negative energy. Otherwise, they may resist the spell."

Hmm. Resistant towels. Definitely not something I would have considered.

Linnea told me the spell to use. Then she stood behind me and put my body in the right position. She showed me where to place my thumb on the wand and demonstrated the tone of voice to use.

"There's way more to this than I thought," I said. "I figured it would be a few magic sentences and poof!"

"It will be, once you're experienced," she said. "In the beginning, it'll require a lot of effort."

I was more than happy to put in the work. The fact that I had this ability at all still astounded me. I had no intention of wasting it.

I aimed the wand at the towels. "Neatly folded, high to low/off to bathrooms, these towels go." I glanced over my shoulder at Linnea. "Don't you usually say the words in Latin?"

"Depends on the spell," she replied. "Beginners are generally better off with spells in English. It feels more natural."

I watched as the neatly stacked towels rose in the air and separated into equal piles before floating out of the room.

"Give them a second, then go and check," Linnea said.

Sure enough, the towels went to their appropriate landing spots. I felt a rush of positive energy.

"Again," I cried. I realized that I sounded an awful lot like Marley.

"It's addictive, isn't it?" Linnea asked, smiling.

"What else can I do for you?" I'd never been so eager to do chores in my life.

"I'll say this much," Linnea told me, giving my shoulder a squeeze. "You're a welcome addition to the family, Ember."

"This isn't hieroglyphics class," Hazel said, scrutinizing my attempt at drawing runes. The-Mistress-of-Runecraft bumped me aside and took my seat. "*This* is how you do it."

"I'm sorry," I said. "I'm tired. I helped Linnea do chores with magic and I'm wiped out." I bit down on my lip to silence myself. I wasn't supposed to mention our extracurricular magic.

Hazel noticed my expression. "I'll keep it to myself. Just don't overdo it. Otherwise, my time here is wasted."

I watched closely as she scribbled the fancy markings on my paper. Her freckled hand moved so quickly, I was sure she was using magic to produce such rapid perfection.

"Good job, Hazel," I said, giving her a pat on the back. "Have you ever considered a career in runecraft?"

"You're hilarious." She handed me the pen. "Sit down and try again."

I begrudgingly complied. "So, if I master telekinesis, will I be able to control this pen with my mind?"

"Probably," she said. "But are you really that lazy?"

I pointed the end of the pen at her. "Watch the insults, Hazel, or I'll tell my aunt you're mistreating her favorite niece."

Hazel fixed me with her crazed clown stare. "And I'll shove that pen so far up your duff, you'll need to master telekinesis to pull it out."

I swallowed hard. "Hazel, have you ever considered moving to New Jersey? I think you'd fit in nicely."

She stretched her bright red lips into a wide smile. "I'd fit in nicely anywhere, Ember. It's my dazzling personality."

"If dazzling means scary in this world, then sure," I muttered, reluctantly turning my attention back to my assignment.

"I heard you were at the Lighthouse for lunch with Sheriff Nash," Hazel said. She stood over me as I worked, and I tried not to be distracted by her peppermint breath.

"I think there's a troll under a bridge that still hasn't heard about my lunch with the sheriff," I said. "Maybe you should run along and tell him."

"He's the young, attractive sheriff and you're the long-lost Rose. It's only natural that tongues are wagging."

"So it's not that *I'm* young and attractive?" I queried.

Hazel pretended to study the runes. "I didn't say you weren't."

I harrumphed like an old man. "The views from the Lighthouse are amazing," I said. "Have you ever been?"

"So, was it a date?" she asked, ignoring my question.

"No, it was lunch." I glanced up at her. "Are we drawing runes today or just gossiping?"

"It's not gossip when it's about yourself," she replied primly.

"Yes, but it's fodder for gossip for *you*."

Hazel huffed and folded her arms. "I'm not a gossip." She stopped. "Fine. Not a *huge* gossip, but your aunt requested that I poke around."

Her answer surprised me. "Why?"

She tapped the paper for me to continue. "I don't know,

but if Hyacinth Rose-Muldoon asks me to do something, I do it."

"Why is that?" I asked. "She's not the head of the coven." That title belonged to the High Priestess, Iris Sandstone.

"She's on the Council of Elders," Hazel said. "Plus, she's a Rose."

"So am I," I said. "That doesn't stop you from bossing me around."

"Your aunt is probably the most powerful witch in Starry Hollow," Hazel said. "You're fortunate that she feels so protective of you. She isn't always so magnanimous."

"Do you know anything about her relationship with my father?" I asked.

Hazel pressed her lips together, debating how to answer. "What would you like to know?"

I shrugged. "Anything, really. I know next to nothing since he never even told me he had a sister."

Hazel's gaze lowered. "Yes, I think that fact hurts your aunt greatly."

"I guess he felt like he was protecting me," I said. From what, I had no idea. Sunday dinner etiquette?

Hazel pulled up a chair. "Your father was a stubborn wizard. He and your aunt were close as children, but butted heads as they grew older, especially when your grandmother died."

My grandmother. So many family members I never knew.

"What was she like?" I'd never had the luxury of knowing any grandparents. I'd thought Marley would be luckier, but her paternal grandparents had been mortified by my out-of-wedlock pregnancy and wanted nothing to do with Karl or us after we told them the news.

"Much like Hyacinth," Hazel said. "Formidable. A good match for your grandfather. He served on the Council of

Elders before your aunt. There's always been a Rose on the council."

"Why did my dad butt heads with Aunt Hyacinth?"

"Those two disagreed about the color of the sky. When he announced his engagement to your mother, Hyacinth was furious that he circumvented the family."

"But she was a member of the same coven," I said. "Isn't that the only thing that matters?"

Hazel inhaled slowly. "Most of the time, but your father was the patriarch of the Rose family at that point. His marriage became a family matter, not an individual choice."

Sheesh. Marriage approval? It was like medieval times in Starry Hollow.

"No wonder Florian rebels," I said. "He's the patriarch now. You'd think my aunt would have learned not to push her will onto stubborn Rose men."

Hazel laughed. "Plenty of stubborn Rose women, too." She gave me a pointed look.

"It feels very last century to be worried about 'appropriate' marriages," I said.

"Get used to it," Hazel said. "No one's overly concerned with my marital prospects, mind you, but I'm not a Rose."

"What? There's no Mister-of-Runecraft?"

"No, there's not." She swatted my leg. "Not that I'd complain if he waltzed into my life."

"Why don't you waltz into his?" I hesitated. "Don't tell me feminism hasn't hit the paranormal world yet."

"Look around you," she said. "There are plenty of women in positions of power here. Anyway, I wouldn't even know where to start." She sighed. "I'm so busy with teaching and private lessons."

"What do you do for fun?" I asked. With her chin-length red hair and freckles, I couldn't imagine Hazel doing much beyond juggling balls and riding a unicycle.

"I play cards."

"That's it?"

"And I do country line dancing at the Shooting Star."

I resisted the urge to gag. "Aren't there nice men that do country line dancing?"

"None that I haven't already banged."

Yikes. So Hazel rode more than a unicycle, apparently. "No long-term prospects?"

"There's one..." She trailed off. "It doesn't matter. Now stop distracting me with personal questions and get back to work."

A knock on the door sent PP3 into a barking frenzy and my pen went flying across the table.

"Pipe down," I said sharply. "It's only the sheriff."

"The sheriff again?" Hazel asked.

I opened the door to greet Sheriff Nash. In his tight jeans and sheriff's hat, he oozed masculinity all over my front step. Inwardly, I warned my body not to betray me. I didn't want the sheriff to know how my stomach dipped at the sight of him. Although he wasn't a mind reader like Alec, he only needed to be a face reader to figure out what I was thinking right now. I wasn't exactly the most adept person at hiding my emotions.

"You okay, Rose?" he asked, with that infuriating lopsided grin of his.

"Of course," I said quickly. "Why wouldn't I be?"

He tilted his head. "You look like you haven't had a meal for days and a big, juicy steak just got slapped on a plate in front of you."

Oops. I adjusted my expression, imagining I was sucking lemons. That should do the trick.

"So you're a detective now, too?" Hazel queried, tucking the Big Book of Scribbles into her bag.

Oh, terrific. Now the sheriff was showing up at the

cottage in front of Hazel. More fodder for gossip.

"I'm a reporter chasing a story," I said. "Aunt Hyacinth's orders." I hoped that invoking my aunt's name would stop the inquisition.

She narrowed her eyes. "Where's he taking you?" Or maybe not.

"To see Artemis Haverford," the sheriff said.

"Artemis?" she gasped. "Spell's bells. Why would you take her there?"

"It's work related," I said.

Hazel appeared skeptical. "Work related? You mean you're going to use her services? I doubt your aunt would approve of Artemis doing the matchmaking for a Rose." She moved to stand between the sheriff and me. "Why in Nature's name are you the one taking her?"

I gave an exasperated sigh. "The sheriff doesn't care whether I find love, Hazel."

"Now, Rose. Don't you believe that for one minute," he replied smoothly. "I'm greatly interested in your love life." He paused. "It has the potential to provide hours of entertainment for me."

I shot him a dirty look. "We're investigating the bachelor frog epidemic," I told Hazel.

Her expression clouded over. "Of course. Florian. It's no wonder she has the paper working on it as well." She turned to look at me. "Mind yourself at Haverford House, Ember. Artemis is an old witch not to be trifled with. You rub her the wrong way, and you'll end up in one of her stews." She hesitated. "She might not even bother to turn you into a frog first."

I gulped. "Thanks for the warning."

I tried to ignore the concern reflected in her crazy clown eyes as she brushed past the sheriff and headed down the walkway.

CHAPTER 7

I JOINED Sheriff Nash in the car and he immediately noticed my pensive mood.

"That time of the month, Rose?" he asked, pulling out of the driveway.

I glanced quickly at him, horrified. "What? No. Why would you say that?"

He chuckled. "I thought nothing was off-limits with you. I believe you're the one who brought it up when we first met."

He was right. The first time I met him was at the station, where Deputy Bolan had driven me to discuss the death of Fleur Montbatten. I had run my mouth in my usual fashion and said more than I probably should have.

"So, what's eating you?" he asked.

I stared out the window as we passed by Thornhold. "Is there any reason to be nervous about meeting Artemis Haverford?"

Understanding crossed his features. "Is this because of what Hazel said?"

"She seemed...concerned. I mean, this witch is just a

matchmaker, right?" A matchmaker that plenty of Starry Hollow residents seemed to visit. How scary could she be?

If Haverford House was any indication, then Artemis was, potentially, very scary indeed. The house was located on the outskirts of town in a secluded wooded area. We drove down a long dirt lane flanked by enormous live oaks. Shards of light filtered through the trees, making me momentarily dizzy.

The red brick front of the house was perfectly symmetrical with two large windows on either side of the portico and three same-sized windows on the second floor. I noticed a widow's walk on the rooftop. Moss and ivy had taken over the façade and a large weeping willow caressed the left side of the house. The wrought iron fence had seen better days. The rusty gate hung askew, begging to be fixed. When I stepped out of the car, an icy wind rushed through me and I shivered.

"People really come here to find a husband or wife?" I suddenly saw the appeal of online dating.

"When you have a reputation as good as Artemis, people are willing to overlook the... ambience," the sheriff said.

"Have you ever paid her a visit?" I asked, as we walked up the pathway to the door.

His brow lifted. "Why? Do I seem like someone who needs the help of a professional?"

I shrugged. "Well, you told me there was no Mrs. Sheriff, and you seemed a little sad about it. I thought maybe you'd exhausted all avenues before giving up."

His brow shot up further, if that was even possible. "Who says I've given up?"

"Oh, so you keep your hair extra scruffy in the hope of attracting the right mate? And you wear your shirts wrinkled hoping that some lovely lady with keen ironing skills will notice and take pity on you?" I nodded sagely. "I see your strategy now."

He bumped me gently with his elbow. "Hey, if we're going to pick on each other, then I have a few pointers for you."

At that moment, the front door opened and the conversation came to a screeching halt.

Artemis Haverford stood before us, wearing a white lace dress yellowed by age. Her bone-white hair was pulled into a severe bun, and her wrinkled skin reminded me of a Bloodhound.

"My, my. Sheriff Granger Nash on my doorstep. To what do I owe the pleasure?" She turned her attention to me. "And you must let me know if you're ever interested in my services, Miss Rose. I would be only too delighted to find you the perfect match."

"You know who I am?" I asked.

The old witch smiled and I caught a glimpse of her rotting teeth. "Course I do, darling. You're the spitting image of your mother."

The sheriff and I exchanged looks.

She stepped to the side. "Do come in. Jefferson will make us a pot of tea."

The wooden floorboards creaked as we followed her into a room that reminded me of Thornhold's parlor. All the windows were covered in heavy drapery so that no sunlight filtered through. The only light emanated from a candlelit chandelier above our heads that was covered in cobwebs.

Artemis sat in a wingback chair, the upholstery riddled with holes. Sheriff Nash and I sat on the settee across from her and I ignored the escaped stuffing that tickled the backs of my knees. Everything in the room was timeworn, from the furniture to the dusty artwork on the walls. I wondered whether she suffered from environment-induced asthma.

A black cat hobbled into the room, looking as ancient and

mangy as its owner. It wouldn't have surprised me in the least to see the cat with a walking stick.

"Come here now, Clementine," Artemis urged. The cat missed on the first jump, but tried again and was rewarded with a warm lap. She eyed us suspiciously before curling up in a ball.

"How sweet," I said. Marley would be all over her.

"Clementine is my familiar," Artemis said. "She has been my constant companion for as long as I can remember."

"My daughter loves cats," I said.

Artemis smiled, flashing those rotten teeth again. "That's the sign of a good witch right there. How about you, Miss Rose? Where do you stand on cats?"

"I try not to stand on them at all," I joked. "It seems to upset them."

Sheriff Nash bit back a laugh. Artemis, on the other hand, showed no signs of possessing a sense of humor.

"I have a dog," I said, my smile fading. "A nine-year-old Yorkie called Prescott Peabody III."

"A big name for such a little dog," Artemis said. Clementine opened one eye and peered at me as if to say, *she means a stupid name.* "I suppose you're here about the influx of frogs."

"You understand why we needed to come and see you," the sheriff said.

A floating tray entered the room with a teapot and three teacups. It drifted down to the sideboard with expert precision.

"Oh, my aunt uses magic like that to serve guests," I said. "She rings little silver bells. She keeps them everywhere in the house." Even in the bathroom for toilet paper emergencies.

I watched as the tea was poured evenly into the cups.

"While I do use magic quite often, this is entirely Jefferson's doing." She glanced at the empty air. "Isn't that right, Jefferson?"

A shiver ran down my spine and I instinctively clutched the sheriff's hand on the settee.

"Um, Miss Haverford. Where exactly is Jefferson?"

She tittered softly. "Why, he's a ghost, of course. He lives in Haverford House with me. He died here under most unfortunate circumstances about a century ago."

I gulped. "What kind of unfortunate circumstances?"

Artemis glanced again at the empty air. "Do you mind if I tell the story, Jefferson?"

A cup of tea sailed into my hand and I balanced it carefully, not wanting to drip the dark liquid onto the light fabric of the settee. Even though nothing was in good shape, I had no desire to contribute to its demise.

"Jefferson was a young man who lived in the house, a nephew of one of my ancestors," Artemis said. "He liked his drink, as many young men do. He was on the roof one day, drinking with friends and showing off the fabulous view to a certain young lady who'd caught his interest. You can see the ocean from the widow's walk. The fool lost his balance and fell from the rooftop, impaling himself on the wrought iron fence below." She took a dainty sip of tea. "He has been part of the house ever since."

"Can you see him?" I asked.

Artemis shook her head. "No, but I sense him acutely. And he is quite adept at moving objects around. He has been my faithful manservant since I was a young witch in this house."

I politely sipped my tea. I was still processing the fact that a ghost had just served it to me.

Artemis set down her teacup and ran her bony fingers through the black fur of her familiar. "Now, on to business, shall we?"

"You said you understood why we'd come to see you," I said. "Is it because you knew that two of the affected men had been to see you recently?"

"There's a bit more to it than that," she replied. "The sheriff knows. I suspect that's the real reason he decided to pay me a visit."

The sheriff drained his teacup and set the empty cup aside. "There is a somewhat famous story about Miss Haverford here in Starry Hollow."

"You mean the fact that she's a matchmaker?" I queried.

"No, darling," Artemis said. "It's the reason I became a matchmaker. *That's* the story." She leaned back in her chair and I noticed the faraway look in her eyes. "I dabbled in transformation spells as a girl. Ever since I got my first wand at eleven years old, I wanted to be an expert in the field. I practiced all the time and had gained quite a reputation by the time I turned eighteen. That's when I met Cedric."

"Cedric Farley was a satyr," Sheriff Nash said. "Part man, part goat."

"Oh, yes," Artemis said. "My family hated the fact that I had fallen hard for a satyr. They wanted me to marry within the coven, of course." She smiled at me. "I'm sure you can relate, darling." She heaved a sigh. "Anyway, I was determined to marry him. My mother said that if we could prove it was true love, then they would give us their blessing. Satyrs tend to have a reputation, you understand. They have an eye for the ladies. Because I dabbled so readily in transformation spells, it seemed only natural that I would turn him into a frog."

My brow creased. "Why a frog?"

"You know the old story, don't you? The kiss of true love turns the frog into a prince," Artemis said. "I was so confident. I changed him into a frog, fully expecting to be able to turn him back with a single kiss."

"So what went wrong?" I asked.

The old witch hesitated and I caught the glimmer of unshed tears in her eyes. "While it was true love for me, it turned out that it wasn't true love for him, after all. I couldn't turn him back into a satyr no matter how much I loved him…because he didn't love me in return."

I gaped at her. "So he was stuck as a frog forever?"

She nodded grimly. "I kept him with me for a while, but he was clearly unhappy. One day, I brought him into the woods and set him free. I like to think that he met another frog that made him happy. I never saw him again."

I felt a rush of sympathy for both of them. "Why do you think he agreed to the transformation spell if he knew he didn't love you?"

Artemis wiped a stray tear from her cheek. "I don't think he knew the truth. I think he believed at the time that he loved me, but it wasn't real. He would have realized it after the fact. But, by then, it would have been too late. I imagine that was the outcome my parents expected."

"They must've felt guilty about Cedric becoming a frog for the rest of his life," I said.

Artemis managed a smile. "You didn't know my parents, darling. Trust me, they felt that he got what he deserved."

Sheriff Nash cleared his throat. "Some folks say that about you, Miss Haverford. That you turned him into a frog as revenge for not loving you. Naturally, having these eligible men in town turned into frogs is reminiscent of your history."

Her gaze dropped to Clementine in her lap. "I understand, Sheriff. But I have no interest in revenge on these men or on anyone else, for that matter. I made my peace with what happened a long time ago. That's the reason I became a matchmaker. I wanted to do better for others than I managed to do for myself."

Artemis inclined her head. "Are you finished with your tea, my dear? I should very much like to read your leaves."

I balked. "My tea leaves? Is that a witch thing?"

"No, it's an art form handed down from generation to generation," she replied, and held out her hand. "Your cup, please."

I handed over my cup and watched as she swirled the cup three times in a counterclockwise direction before draining the liquid onto her saucer. She peered into the cup and shifted around the remaining contents, staring intently.

"Is this part of the matchmaking service?" I asked. "Do you use tea leaves to help you find partners for your clients?"

"Sometimes," Artemis said. "It depends." She continued to fixate on the leaves. "Very interesting symbols. Not that I am the least bit surprised."

I leaned forward and peered into the cup, where I saw only brown globs. "They look like dirty clouds."

Sheriff Nash laughed. "That makes sense. The Ancient Celts used clouds to tell the future."

"And the past and present, too," Artemis added.

"The most interesting shapes I ever saw in the clouds were a dolphin and a chicken," I said.

"Our stories are everywhere if we choose to see them," Artemis said. She bowed her head and studied the tea leaves again. "A broom."

"Well, that's easy," I said. "I rode one recently."

"It's not a literal interpretation," Artemis said. "A broom signifies a change in your life."

I rolled my eyes. "No kidding."

Artemis clapped her hands. "Ah, a daisy. Delightful."

"No rose, huh?" I queried. Aunt Hyacinth would be *so* disappointed.

"A daisy means happiness in love, darling, so I suppose

you won't need my services after all." She peered at the contents again and frowned.

"What is it?" I asked. "Did the petals fall off?" That would be just my luck.

"Armor," Artemis said. "It means you'll face difficulties and dangers." She looked up and smiled. "But that you will face them with courage."

Courage was cool, but I wasn't so excited by the 'difficulties and dangers' part.

"How difficult and dangerous are we talking?" I asked. "Like death and destruction, or trying to snag the last cookie on bingo night at the senior citizens complex?"

Artemis pressed her wrinkled lips together. "Hard to say. The leaves don't give details. They're not a road map, darling."

"What about the sheriff?" I asked, nodding toward him. "Can you read his?"

Sheriff Nash waved us off. "No, no. I like my future unknown. It's more fun that way."

"As you wish, Sheriff," Artemis said.

"You'd think with Jefferson around, the house wouldn't be so dark and musty," I said. "Maybe he can help you with the cleaning or run a load of laundry once in a while."

Sheriff Nash shot me a horrified look.

"What?" I asked. "We're supposed to pretend? This house is like an abandoned museum and she's dressed like the bride of Frankenstein. I'm shocked that anyone would come out here to deliver pizza, let alone find a soulmate."

Sheriff Nash buried his face in his hands. "Stars and stones, Rose. I think I know the real reason you came to Starry Hollow. You were deemed too obnoxious for New Jersey."

"That's a pretty high bar," I said.

Artemis laughed gently. "I take no offense. To be honest, I haven't had a breath of air as fresh as her in over fifty years."

"I'll take your word for it," he said.

"See?" I told him, pointing to myself. "Fresh air."

"I'm sorry I couldn't be of more help with the frog situation," Artemis said. "I do take pride in serving the community when I'm able."

"You just keep doing what you're doing, Artemis," the sheriff said. "That's contribution enough."

"You're welcome back anytime, either one of you," Artemis said. "If you decide you'd like to pursue a match, I'm happy to help."

"I might just take you up on that," I said.

The sheriff glanced at me in disbelief. "She saw a daisy, Rose. What's the rush?"

I shrugged. "No rush. Maybe that's how I find happiness in love. The tea leaves don't actually say I don't get help."

"Good luck with your investigation," Artemis said, and closed the door behind us.

The second we were out of earshot, Sheriff Nash shot me an inquisitive look. "Are you really considering her services?"

"Great balls of sweet baby Elvis, no," I said. "But as soon as I have a spare couple of hours, I'm going back there with a cleaning crew and a glam squad. It's high time Artemis Haverford finds a match of her own."

CHAPTER 8

MARLEY INSISTED on being a good cousin and paying Florian a visit after school. Apparently, she'd started a unit on pond life in science class and was convinced that Florian was going to die if we kept him in the glass container for too long.

Simon guided us to the parlor, where Florian's enclosure was set on a sideboard in front of the window.

"At least he has a view," I said.

"Yes, his mother was quite insistent on it," Simon said, before retreating to another room. I wondered whether he was heeding the call of a silent silver bell.

"I feel horrible," Marley said. "He looks so unhappy in there." She tapped on the glass and waved to him. The frog simply stared back at her.

"I don't think he feels happiness or unhappiness right now," I said. "He's a frog."

Marley cast me a sidelong glance. "You don't think frogs feel emotions?"

I shrugged. "Don't think so. I guess we can ask him when he's turned back into a wizard."

"That's optimistic," Marley said. "If no one figures out who's doing this, Florian might be stuck as a frog forever."

I immediately thought of Cedric, the unfortunate satyr, and my stomach twisted. "No one's going to let that happen," I said. "You forget your Aunt Hyacinth is cracking the whip on this case."

Marley leaned her elbows on the sideboard, resting her chin on her knuckles. "Can't we just take him out for a little while so he can get fresh air? A frog doesn't belong trapped in a glass container."

"I don't know, Marley," I said. "I think he's safer in here."

"We'll just let him stretch his legs and catch a few flies," she insisted. "You're always encouraging me to get outside and take my nose out of a book. Here's your big chance."

Whoa. Marley was playing the Mom card against me. Clever girl.

"Fine," I relented. "We'll take him out for half an hour. But you have to keep him in your pocket. I'm not touching any mucous coating."

Marley eagerly retrieved Florian from the glass enclosure. She stroked his green head with her thumb. "Don't worry, Florian. We'll take good care of you." She placed the frog carefully in her pocket.

"Let's go, before someone catches us," I said. The last thing I needed was to be on Aunt Hyacinth's bad side. She'd probably turn me into a fly just for spite.

We snuck out of the main house and made our way toward the woods that bordered the estate.

"There's a pond back here," Marley said. "I saw it when I took PP3 for a walk the other day."

"Now that you mention him, he's due to go out," I said. "Why don't I get him and meet you at the pond?"

Marley's eyes shone with excitement. "You'd let me take Florian on my own?"

"Of course." Any time Marley showed a shred of independence, I was all over it like the sheriff on cracklewhip chowder.

"Once you walk past the gate," Marley instructed, "walk about twenty feet and then go left. There's a path there that leads to the pond."

I gave her a thumbs up and trotted toward the cottage. The dog was waiting by the door, as though he knew I was on the way. I grabbed his leash and hooked it to his collar before heading back out. Secretly, I was glad that Marley had suggested an outdoor excursion. I'd discovered that the mixture of salty and fresh air that Starry Hollow provided gave me renewed energy. I felt the way I did after a productive day—energized and positive. This little trip to the pond wasn't just for Florian's sake, it was for all of us.

Halfway there, the dog stopped to pee, and I took a moment to admire the grounds of the estate. Some days I still had to pinch myself. I couldn't believe that I lived here now. My life in New Jersey seemed so far away. I wondered whether Hilda Santiago had found a repo replacement for me. I still felt guilty for leaving her in the lurch, but I didn't really have a choice. When a trio of coven cousins show up in your apartment via a magical wormhole and kick the bad guy's derrière, you follow their orders. I knew in my heart that Hilda would understand.

I passed the gate and walked the required twenty feet until I saw the path. PP3 seemed to stop and sniff every single leaf and berry that we passed. He took 'leisurely stroll' to a whole new level. By the time we made it to the pond, Florian was hopping around on lily pads like a kid in a bouncy castle.

Marley gave me a triumphant look. "See? This was a great idea. He loves it."

"He'll probably never want to speak of it again, once he's turned back into a wizard," I said.

"It doesn't matter," Marley said. "We're giving him a little bit of happiness now while he's stuck as a frog, and that's what's important."

I was inclined to agree. I'd want someone to pay attention to me if I were in his shoes...or his frog legs.

After losing interest in a stick, PP3 caught sight of Florian skirting the edge of the pond and began to bark. He tugged on the leash, straining to be set free.

"No," I said firmly. "No frog." We didn't need PP3 to mistake Florian for prey. Despite the Yorkie's age, he still liked to chase things.

Florian hopped to a lily pad in the middle of the pond and stared at us.

"I think PP3 upset him," Marley said. "He doesn't want to hop anymore."

"He's probably afraid to get too close to the dog," I said. Not that I blamed him. The Yorkie was small but fierce. He definitely had a Napoleon complex.

The frog hopped again and PP3 began to bark wildly.

"No bark," I said. The Yorkie ignored me and continued to focus on the frog.

"Mom," Marley gasped. "Florian is hopping away to the other side of the pond."

Sure enough, Florian was making his away across the lily pads to the opposite side of the pond. Marley began to run along the perimeter, calling his name.

"Marley, you have to catch him," I said. I worked quickly to tie PP3's leash around the base of a tree so that I could help Marley go after our wayward cousin.

Marley made it around the pond just as Florian hopped onto land and disappeared between two bushes.

"Mom, use magic," Marley called.

I waved my hands in the air helplessly. "What kind of magic will stop a frog from hopping away?"

Marley didn't know either. Together, we scoured the area, searching for signs of Florian.

"This is very, very bad," Marley said. When she looked up at me, I saw that her eyes were brimming with tears.

"It'll be okay," I said. "We'll find him." I retrieved PP3 and walked him around the area to sniff for Florian. After an hour, I told Marley it was time to call it quits.

"This is all my fault," Marley said, sniffling.

I put a comforting arm around her shoulders. "You were doing a nice thing for Florian. He chose to hop away and hide. Don't worry." I kissed her forehead. "We'll figure something out."

When we edged around the pond to head back to the cottage, there were three frogs on lily pads.

Marley gasped. "Mom, do you think one of them is Florian?"

"It's possible." But I had no earthly idea. "We need to take one of them with us no matter what." We had to put a frog—any frog—back in the glass enclosure before Aunt Hyacinth noticed Florian was missing.

Marley studied the three frogs, her nose scrunching. "They all look the same."

"That's racist," I said. "Now pick one."

Marley reached for the frog on the closest lily pad and managed to snag it before it could hop away. She stuffed it into her pocket, its legs flailing wildly.

"Let's go," I said hurriedly.

I waited outside the house with PP3, while Marley crept inside to deliver the frog to the glass enclosure.

"Did anyone see you?" I asked, when she emerged outside.

"Only Simon, and I told him I'd taken Florian for a walk."

Phew.

"How can we tell we've got the right frog?" she asked. "The only way to know whether it's Florian is if he turns back into himself when the curse is broken."

"I imagine the spell will break no matter where he is," I said. "So if he's in the woods, he'll turn back into Florian there." At least, I hoped so.

"Shouldn't we look for him tomorrow?" she asked, as we walked back to the cottage.

"We don't know that it's not him in the house," I said. "We'd have to collect all the frogs around the pond and wait to see which one turns out to be Florian." And that plan seemed like a recipe for disaster.

Marley wiped a tear from her cheek. "Can we have chicken nuggets for dinner tonight?"

Ah, the breaded food group—a ten-year-old's comfort food.

"Absolutely," I said, and held her hand all the way home.

After possibly losing Florian to the call of the wild, I decided I needed a night out. I remembered Aster's mention of the Whitethorn and convinced Linnea to join me.

The Whitethorn was straight out of *Lord of the Rings*. I half expected a hobbit to come stumbling out after one too many pints. The white building had a thatched roof and a rounded wooden door.

"Thanks for coming with me," I said to Linnea.

"Are you kidding?" She smiled brightly. "Do you know how infrequently I leave the inn? Thank you for giving me a legitimate excuse to make myself presentable." Presentable was an understatement. The Rose-Muldoon siblings were all stunning—Linnea could turn heads wearing a potato sack.

"I'm glad Bryn and Hudson are willing to entertain Marley at the inn," I said.

Linnea laughed. "I have a feeling Marley will be the one babysitting them by bedtime. They argue nonstop."

I followed Linnea through the door of the pub and noticed the wide wooden planks beneath our feet as we approached the bar. They looked old and well worn. The interior was dark, with wooden beams that stretched across the low ceiling. Behind the bar was a man in a yellow jacket, a black pirate's hat, and, of course, an eye patch.

"Good evening, ladies," he said. "Captain Yellowjacket is here to attend to all your spirituous needs."

"Thanks, Duncan," Linnea said.

He cleared his throat loudly. "It's Captain Yellowjacket, remember?"

Linnea turned to me. "Duncan claims to be a direct descendant of Captain Blackfang, the famous vampire pirate."

"Not as impressive as being the descendant of the One True Witch," Captain Yellowjacket said. "But it's my claim to fame."

A red and blue parrot appeared seemingly from nowhere to land on the bartender's shoulder.

"Let me guess," I said. "This is your faithful companion, Polly?"

The parrot cocked its head. "The name's Bittersteel."

"That sounds more like a sword than a parrot," I said.

"If you want to see something long and dangerous," the parrot squawked, "I'd be happy to show you."

Crap on a stick. A smutty parrot?

"Stop being such a dirty birdie," Captain Yellowjacket chastised him, and I caught a glimpse of the bartender's fangs. Yep, definitely a vampire pirate. "I don't want you scaring off new customers."

"I think it's your putrid breath that usually does that," the parrot said.

"What can I get you to drink, love?" Captain Yellowjacket asked.

Linnea rested her forearms on the counter. "A damson sparkle, please. Straight up."

"How about you, luscious lips?" Bittersteel squawked.

Luscious lips? That was a new one for me. "I'll have an ale. Whatever's on tap."

"She's easy," Captain Yellowjacket said. "I like that in a customer."

"And I like that in a woman," Bittersteel added.

I groaned. "You're a parrot. The only thing you like in a woman is the crackers in her handbag."

Captain Yellowjacket roared with laughter. "She's got you there, Bittersteel." He fixed Linnea's drink first before pulling my pint.

"So, I heard this place is old and magical with gold in the basement," I said, accepting the glass. "Is any of it actually true?"

"Oh, it's the history of the Whitethorn you're after?" Captain Yellowjacket appeared pleased.

"You love telling this story, don't you?" I asked.

He rubbed his hands together. "What's not to love?" He leaned forward. "Unless you're after the gold. Then I'll need to use my fangs as a warning to you."

"I'm not after your gold," I assured him, "but I'd like to know more about it."

He straightened and poured himself a shot. Then he smacked his lips together and prepared to speak. "Once upon a time…"

"It's a fairy tale?" I asked. "I thought it was a history lesson."

He pointed a long, yellow fingernail at me. "Don't interrupt, witch. It's not a fairy tale, but I like to start the story that way."

"Sorry. Please go on," I said. I straightened in my seat and zipped my lip.

"Once upon a time, there was a grand ship called the Ancient Mariner. They sailed from port to port, the good captain and his crew, until the night a vicious storm rolled across the sea and dragged the Ancient Mariner on to the shore of a strange island."

"Manhattan?" I quipped.

He gave me the stink eye before continuing. "The island was full of creatures that looked and talked like humans, except for their noticeable fangs and their insatiable taste for blood."

I gulped. "Long Island then?"

Bittersteel gave me a threatening look and I backed down. I didn't trust that beak.

"The captain and his crew were kept as vampire slaves for many years before they were finally turned. That's when the good captain exacted his revenge. He murdered every vampire on the island, saved his crew, and returned to the high seas on the Ancient Mariner as a vampire pirate."

"That's Captain Blackfang?" I asked.

"Aye," Captain Yellowjacket said. "He sailed at night until he found a witch in Greece willing to charm the ship, so that he and his crew could travel in sunlight."

"And that's when they became feared and revered?" I asked.

"They plundered countless towns along the coast, leaving a trail of destruction in their wake. Captain Blackfang gained a reputation as the most fearsome vampire pirate that ever lived and died and lived again. Legend has it they arrived in the dead of night on the shores of Starry Hollow and hid their treasures in various places around the town before heading back to sea a few days later."

"But they haven't come back?" I asked.

Captain Yellowjacket shook his head. "No one is brave enough to seek the treasure, in case one day Captain Black-fang returns to claim it. There's even talk of vials of enchanted blood that would give the gift of immortality without the need for vampirism."

"That would be worth a fortune," I said.

"Aye," Captain Yellowjacket said. "It certainly would."

"I guess that's why the tourist board doesn't use the story to promote the town," I said. "They're afraid of being swarmed by treasure hunters."

"Tourists learn the story when they come," Linnea said, "but it's not a story we exploit."

"I thought there was gold under the Whitethorn," I said.

The captain shrugged. "Maybe. Maybe not. Who knows?"

"So how are you a direct descendant?" I asked.

"His last visit to Starry Hollow was a few days," he replied. "Long enough to meet a lovely vampire lass called Marla and leave her with a precious treasure of her own."

My eyes widened. "You're actually his son?"

"I am," he said, puffing out his chest.

"So is Marla still around?" I asked.

"She moved to a paranormal town outside Boca Raton about ten years ago," he said. "She's partial to the climate there."

"You've got to be kidding me," Linnea grumbled.

My head jerked toward my cousin. "What's the matter?"

"Darling ex-wife, what brings your sweet lips to my watering hole?" Wyatt Nash sauntered up to the bar, looking like his usual sexy werewolf self in a tight gray T-shirt and dark jeans. He was about two inches shorter than his brother, but wore his brown hair about two inches longer.

"They're all your watering holes," she replied crisply. "If I tried to avoid the places you drank, I'd be limited to my own kitchen." She paused. "No, wait. You drink there, too, even when I've asked you to stop."

Wyatt draped an arm across her shoulders and she tried to shake him off.

"Wyatt, I can smell the ale on your breath. Please take your hand off me or you know what will happen."

He grinned at her. "You know I like it when you play rough."

Linnea's jaw tightened. "Wyatt Nash, I'm warning you right now. Remove that grubby paw from my shoulder or I'll do it for you."

He squeezed her shoulder. "By the gods, I love it when you boss me around. Sometimes when I'm alone in bed at night..."

She snorted. "That's a lie right there. You're never alone in bed."

"Don't be jealous, my beautiful rose. You know I only have eyes for you."

As he leaned in to plant a kiss her cheek, Linnea reacted. With the flick of her wrist, Wyatt's face jerked backward and his body went sailing across the room. Amazingly, he landed on his feet, completely balanced.

"Stupid werewolf genes," she muttered.

Wyatt's grin only broadened. "You know I still love you, Linnea," he yelled.

"You have a funny way of showing it," she called back, before turning her attention back to her cocktail. "Sorry about that, Ember."

"Don't apologize to me," I said. "I'm sorry he torments you."

She offered a vague smile. "I admit, sometimes I find it more irresistible than I should."

"Makes sense to me. You loved him."

"Still do, if I'm being honest," she said. "But I know it will never work between us. I need a faithful man and Wyatt isn't programmed for fidelity."

"Because of the werewolf genes?" I asked.

She examined me. "Why? You worried about Granger?"

"What? No, of course not." I felt the heat rush to my cheeks. "I was curious about werewolves in general."

She ignored my protest. "Listen, Granger Nash is as wonderful as they come. If I'd been a smart witch, I'd have fallen in love with him instead."

Her comment reminded me of a question I'd been meaning to ask her. "Do you know the history between Alec Hale and the sheriff? Why do they despise each other so much?"

Linnea sucked in a breath. "Those two have never been friendly. There's unspoken competition between them."

"Because of the usual tension between werewolves and vampires?" I queried.

She shook her head. "No, it's more than that with those two. Wyatt told me once that they'd fought over a woman."

Ah. That explained a lot. "Any clue who she is?"

"All I remember is that she left town a few years ago with a centaur. Rode off into the sunset on his back."

"Ouch." I winced. "So they both lost out to a centaur?"

"Apparently." Linnea finished her drink. "Ready for another one?"

"Just one more," I said. "I have my first official psychic skills class tomorrow, so I need to be sharp. The assessment left me practically comatose." I couldn't imagine what effect the class itself would have.

"At least you have potential in several areas," Linnea said. "That's exciting. We could use a telepath in the family, if for no other reason than to know what Mother is really thinking."

I shuddered at the idea of eavesdropping on Aunt

Hyacinth's thoughts. What if I accidentally forged a psychic link with Simon?

"I don't think anyone should shoulder that burden alone," I said.

Linnea laughed. "You're too right."

CHAPTER 9

FOR MY FIRST official psychic skills lesson, Marigold accompanied me into the woods behind Rose Cottage.

"Should I be leaving a trail of breadcrumbs?" I asked. I ducked my head to avoid the Spanish moss hanging from a low branch. "Are you leading me to a gingerbread house or something?"

Marigold stepped over a wayward branch and stopped in the middle of a small clearing. "The woodland creatures would eat the breadcrumbs. You'd need to use ribbons on tree branches or something indigestible."

"If I ever get lost in the forest, I hope it's with you," I said.

"I think it's best to practice something like telekinesis in the great outdoors."

"You mean isolated in the woods so that I don't hurt anyone," I said.

"That may also play a role," Marigold replied primly.

I wasn't offended, although I doubted I could do much damage when I could barely shift a feather more than an inch.

"The woods are so different here," I observed. Although I

hadn't spent much time in the woods in New Jersey, Starry Hollow had trees and shrubs I'd never seen before.

"Some of what you see here is the result of being in a paranormal town," Marigold explained. "Other bits, like the Spanish moss and the live oaks, are because you're in the South. They don't grow up north. They like a hot, humid climate."

"My father talked about live oaks," I said. "For someone who lived in suburban sprawl, he knew a lot of stories about trees."

"As any good wizard does," Marigold said.

I'd never questioned his knowledge. He was a fountain of random information. I realized too late that I should have paid closer attention. Asked more questions. I felt like I'd squandered my limited time with him.

"So all these berries that I haven't heard of, like burstberries," I said. "They're magical fruits?"

Marigold nodded. "There are many things here that aren't available in the human world."

I was surprised some enterprising paranormal or human hadn't found a way to make money on a magical black market.

"Okay, so what's my first lesson?" I asked. "Complete deforestation?"

"That would be both ridiculous and not environmentally friendly," Marigold said. "Silver Moon witches get their magical energy from Nature. It would be self-destruction."

Good to know.

Marigold surveyed the area. "We'll start small. I'd like to see you move that leaf." She pointed to a hand-shaped leaf on the ground in front of me.

"How will we know if I moved it or if the wind did it?" I asked.

"If you're good enough, eventually, you'll get to the point

where the wind did it because you controlled the wind," she said.

As crazy as it sounded, I knew it was possible. After all, the whole reason I was here now was because I'd managed to make it rain in order to save my life.

"So I need to focus my will on the leaf, right?" I asked.

"That's right," she said. "Pour all your concentration and focus into that single leaf. Will it to move. It's best to open your eyes when you do so."

"I thought closing my eyes would help minimize distractions," I said.

"That's why we're out here in the woods," Marigold said. "There's no dog or modern amenities to draw your attention."

Fair enough. I plopped on the ground in front of the leaf and stared. I felt ridiculous and I wondered what Hilda would say if she could see me now, sitting in the dirt and making crazy eyes at a leaf.

I wasn't sure how long to give it before I decided the effort was a failure. The longer I concentrated, the longer the leaf remained unmoving. In fact, it seemed like the wind had died down just to spite me.

After a few minutes, I glanced up at Marigold. "Keep going?"

"Keep going," she agreed.

"What on earth?" I noticed that she was fiddling with a familiar object. "Are you playing with a Rubik's Cube?"

"Yes," she said, brightening. "Have you ever done one of these?"

"Definitely," I said. "My father was a huge fan of the 80s. Music, television, toys like that one."

Marigold continued moving the puzzle around, trying to complete the yellow side. "I find it soothing when I want to keep my mind occupied."

"Where did you get it?" I asked.

"The shops here carry toys and games from the human world," Marigold said. "It isn't only magical toys."

I returned my attention to the leaf. I remembered my father showing me how to solve the Rubik's Cube. I suspect he liked it for the same reasons as Marigold. It helped him to focus on one thing and block out distractions. Now that I knew a little more about him, I figured it was a coping mechanism to keep his thoughts from wandering to dark places.

I pretended the leaf was a Rubik's Cube and that my sole purpose in life was to solve the puzzle. I brought forth my will and thought of nothing else in the world except moving the leaf. I felt small jolts as the leaf slid across the ground.

I glanced up quickly. "Did you see that? It moved at least a foot."

Marigold peered down at the leaf. "How do you know it wasn't the wind? Remember my breath on the feather?"

"For one thing, there's no breeze right now. And for another thing, I felt it."

Marigold's hands dropped to her sides. "What do you mean, you felt it?"

I tried to describe the jolt. "It was like the inside of my body jumped a little bit, just like the leaf."

Marigold's thin lips stretched into a smile. "Very good. Now do it again."

"The same thing?"

"Yes," she said. "One more time to make sure it wasn't a fluke. Then we'll move on to the next lesson."

I followed her instructions and moved the leaf again. I felt the same small jolt and knew that I'd been successful.

"Now I want you to make the acorn fall off the branch," she said, pointing.

The acorn was heavier than the leaf, but still seemed to be manageable. I sat cross-legged in front of the branch and follow the same mental pattern as I had with the leaf. After three attempts, I gave a groan of exasperation.

"Don't get discouraged," Marigold said. "Although it seems counterintuitive, mental exercises like these can wipe you out more than physical exertion."

"My cousin said something similar," I said. "Linnea said that magic drains you when you use a lot of it."

"Very true," Marigold said. "Even highly experienced witches lose energy when they've used too much magic. It's always important to recharge. It will be hard for you in the beginning. Your body and mind are still learning how to work together."

I concentrated on the acorn. I wanted to be able to tell Marley that I'd managed both the leaf and the acorn today. And, of course, I wanted to reap the benefit of a Mom joke involving the acorn not falling far from the tree.

"I can sense your distraction," Marigold said. "Empty your mind of all other thoughts. The only things that exist in the world right now are you and the acorn. Nothing else."

She fell silent and I concentrated fully on moving the acorn. I felt another jolt and watched as it rolled to the side of the branch. Then gravity took control and the acorn plummeted to the earth.

"Well done, Ember," she said, and I heard the note of pride in her voice.

"That was fun," I said. "Can I do it again?"

"Absolutely," Marigold said. "Three cheers for you."

As long as she didn't *actually* do three cheers, I was fine. I placed the acorn back on the branch and managed to make it fall again. My heart was racing with excitement. I was an achiever! Who knew?

"What's next?" I asked. "That?" I pointed to a nearby stick.

Marigold shook her head gently. "I think that's enough for one lesson. I can see that you're growing weary."

"I'm not getting tired," I objected, and moved to pull myself to my feet. I stumbled and fell back to the ground, slamming my bottom on the hard ground.

Marigold smirked. "You were saying?"

"But I barely did anything," I said. "A leaf and an acorn? They're so light."

"Trust me, Ember," she said. "Your body is telling you to rest. Sit for a moment before we return to the cottage."

I remained seated on the ground, trying to steady my breathing. She was right. I felt like I'd overdone it.

"So what kind of cool things am I going to be able to do once I build up my abilities?" I pictured myself throwing lightning bolts and swinging trees like baseball bats.

Marigold tucked the Rubik's Cube into her cloak pocket. "Why would you want to cause destruction when it's so much better to create beauty?"

Popcorn balls. I was too tired to shield my thoughts.

"I wouldn't really do any of those things," I said. "It's just a silly fantasy. Like telling off a crappy boss or getting revenge on an ex-boyfriend with itching powder."

Marigold inhaled deeply and centered herself. She moved her hand gracefully in front of her in a circular motion. Her movements were mesmerizing and a sense of peace over- whelmed me. Leaves began to float in the air, bowing to her silent commands. One by one, they danced in front of her, creating an outline of some kind. More leaves drifted to join the others until the shape was completely filled in. She'd created an image of a tree using the leaves that had fallen from it.

"It's beautiful," I said. "But what's the point?"

Marigold's concentration broke and the leaves fell to the ground in a pile. "Why does there have to be a point? Have you ever heard of art for art's sake?"

Not really. "I'll be able to make leaves dance around? I guess that's pretty cool."

Marigold came over and helped me to my feet. "This is only the beginning, Ember Rose. I promise you'll be able to do more than that. Much more."

CHAPTER 10

I WAS MASSAGING the cramp in my hand after drawing one too many runes for homework when a knock on the door startled me. PP3 ran to the door and gave it a hard sniff before deciding not to bark.

"No barking?" I queried. "Now I'm intrigued."

Simon stood on the front step in full butler gear. "Good day, Miss Rose. My lady would like to see you in her office posthaste."

"Don't you have a phone?" I asked. "Did that relentless taskmaster make you walk all the way out here in your fancy clothes?"

Simon's expression remained blank. "I enjoy a good walk, miss. It keeps the blood flowing."

"If you say so," I said.

We left the cottage and traipsed across the grounds toward the main house.

"Why do you call her 'my lady,' but she calls you by your first name?"

"Your aunt is the lady of the house," Simon replied. "She

asked for my preference many years ago and I answered her truthfully."

"Am I in trouble? Is she mad that I haven't figured out who put the spell on Florian yet? Because I swear I'm working on it." More importantly, has she figured out that the frog in the house may not be Florian? My palms began to sweat.

"It is not for me to speculate, miss," he said.

"So, do you have set working hours or are you at her beck and call?" I asked, trying to distract myself with idle chitchat. "Because you're always around."

"I live at Thornhold, but my lady is more than generous," Simon said.

"Do her silver bells annoy you?" I asked. "When you hear one now, do you just want to throw it across the room and smash it to pieces?"

He hesitated. "I have no such desire, miss. The enchanted bells assist me in serving my lady. I happen to enjoy being excellent at my job."

No argument from me there. Simon was an incredible butler, not that I had experience in such matters. My closest brush with a butler before now was playing Clue with Marley.

We arrived at the house and Simon led me to Aunt Hyacinth's office.

I looked around eagerly. "Bonus! I haven't gotten to see this room yet."

"If you have a seat, my lady will be with you shortly."

I made myself comfortable in one of the leather chairs and waited for my aunt. The room seemed more like a library than an office. The walls were lined with bookshelves and a large mahogany desk sat in the middle of the room. The windows behind the desk provided a view of the grounds to the east. I imagined the view looked amazing when the sun rose in the morning.

"Thank you for coming so quickly, dear," Aunt Hyacinth said, stepping into the office. She wore a golden kaftan that reminded me of an Indian sari. Her white-blond hair was pulled back in a French twist.

"It didn't seem like I had much of a choice," I said. "When Simon shows up on your doorstep in his fat tie, it's like the Terminator saying 'come with me if you want to live.'"

Aunt Hyacinth frowned. Not a *Terminator* fan, apparently.

"His fat tie is called an ascot," she said.

Noted.

My aunt took her place behind the desk and steepled her fingers. "I understand you've been diligently following up leads on Florian's case."

Although she didn't seem to suspect anything about the frog in the enclosure, something about her approach set off my alarm bells. "Yes, isn't that what you wanted?"

Aunt Hyacinth gave me a reassuring smile. "Yes, yes. Of course, my darling. I'm just surprised the sheriff would let you tag along so often during his investigation. I assumed you'd be working with Alec and Bentley. It's so unlike Granger to show a modicum of sense."

I shrugged. "He's been pretty sensible as far as I can tell," I said. "He said that he knew I'd be talking to people whether he wanted me to or not, so we may as well talk to them together."

"What about Bentley?"

"We decided to divide and conquer, for the most part."

She sat in silence for a moment, considering me. "I understand you and the sheriff had lunch together at the Lighthouse the other day."

Sheesh. My aunt really had a bee in her bonnet over this lunch.

"It was after we spoke with Dakota Musgrove, one of the suspects," I explained. "She's a chef there, and she'd been on dates with all three frogs." I shook my head. "I don't mean that she dated the frogs. Obviously, she dated the men."

Aunt Hyacinth held up a hand. "I'm following you just fine, dear. I'm interested in why you felt the need to encourage him."

My brain buzzed. "Encouraged him to do what? I don't follow."

Aunt Hyacinth sighed. "It took how many years for Linnea to realize that she made a huge mistake with Wyatt? I don't intend to repeat the same mistake with you."

I laughed. "I'm not about to marry the sheriff and have his werewolf pups."

"Not today, naturally," Aunt Hyacinth said. "But this is how it begins. An innocent lunch, and then suddenly you're choosing the date for your elopement and trying to find a way to hide your werewolf pregnancy."

So that was what this was really about. She was concerned that she would have another Linnea and Wyatt on her hands.

"Aunt Hyacinth, the lunch was business. I have no interest in dating Sheriff Nash, and I'm pretty sure he has no interest in dating me. At best, he finds me annoying."

"Well, that's absurd," Aunt Hyacinth said. "If anyone's annoying around here, it's those Nash brothers. They need to learn to steer clear of the witches in this town."

I bit back a smile. "I appreciate your concern, but, as Marley will tell you, I have no interest in dating. At all." It suddenly occurred to me that I should tell her about Ben before she misconstrued that outing as well. "On that note, you should probably know that I agreed to let an elf take me out tomorrow night. His name is Ben and he owns Snips-n-Clips. The sheriff and I went to talk to him about the frog situation and he offered to show me around town."

Aunt Hyacinth gave me an appraising look. "An elf, did you say?"

"I'm more interested in making friends than boyfriends, so I'm not interested in dating him," I said, "but, if I were, I'd still go out with him, whether you approved or not. I know you want me to be like Aster and marry a wizard and have magical Rose babies, but I don't know yet whether that's my path. If it is, great, but it won't be because you insisted on it." I met her steely gaze. "Are we clear on that?"

She continued to stare at me a bit longer, probably waiting for me to look away first. I wasn't going to play that game.

"I see," she finally said. "You're as stubborn as your father, I'll say that for you."

"He would have liked that," I said.

Aunt Hyacinth stood and escorted me to the door. "I didn't say it was a compliment, darling."

It would have unnerved Aunt Hyacinth to know that I was joining the sheriff on another interview shortly after the meeting in her office. Between the security around Thornhold and the rumor mill, she probably knew the moment I got into his car.

As we drove into town, he displayed that irritating habit of repeatedly hitting the button to change the radio station. I could barely catch the tune of the song before he switched to the next song.

"Do I need to buy you a fidget spinner?" I practically shouted. I was sorely tempted to slap his hand away from the radio controls, sheriff or not.

He cast a sidelong glance at me. "What?"

"How can you tell what song options are on if you keep flipping past them?"

He grinned. "When I hear one I like, I'll stop."

"But you can't hear anything," I insisted. "One note tells you nothing. If this is the strategy you've applied to dating, it's no wonder you're still single."

His expression clouded over. "That's harsh, Rose." He placed his hand back on the steering wheel. "Go on. You choose."

I hit the button twice before the thumping chords of *Born in the USA* grabbed my attention.

"Springsteen," I cheered.

"You're a fan, huh?"

"It's a state requirement," I replied. "Plus, my father loved this song. It's from the 80s." I could still remember playing my air guitar in the kitchen with him.

The sheriff bobbed his head. "I guess I can see the appeal."

"You guess?" I asked, outraged. "We may need to part ways right here, Sheriff Nash."

"You'll have to check out some of the local bands now that you're an official resident," he said. "The Wishing Well hosts a lot of live music."

"How is paranormal music different from human music?"

He parked the car on Bailiwick Road right in front of our destination. "The music isn't much different, but you haven't lived until you've seen a guy with horns and a tail strumming a six string."

"I look forward to crossing it off my bucket list." I glanced up at the name of the shop—Charmed, I'm Sure. "Who's the next suspect?"

"Bryony Pennywhistle. She owns this shop."

"Got it. Let's go, partner."

He tipped back his hat and stared at me. "Partner?"

"Yeah, you know, like in cop shows."

"I don't watch cop shows."

I strolled up to the shop door. "Maybe you should. You might learn something." Although I didn't look back, I could feel his scowl and a laugh churned inside me.

I entered the shop and was immediately struck by the rows upon rows of colorful bottles in all shapes and sizes. Definitely not the right place to practice my telekinesis.

I shot him a quick look. "Potions?"

"Didn't the name of the store give it away?" he asked.

"I didn't really notice." I frowned. "So, she's a..."

"A witch," Bryony said, appearing behind the counter. She was oddly beautiful. Her cropped hair was dyed a pale pink and her eyes were large and violet. I wondered whether she drank one of the store's potions to achieve her look. "I'm not big on attending coven meetings, though. Never been much of a team player, much to my parents' chagrin."

"She sounds right up your alley, Rose," the sheriff said, jostling me with his elbow.

"Rose?" Bryony considered me with interest. "You're Ember Rose?"

"So says my Starry Hollow passport." The all-access pass to the town's offerings.

She studied me intently. "I see the resemblance, although it's subtle. You don't look like the usual carbon copy."

"I don't understand," I said, with a small shake of my head. "You can't be a witch."

Bryony looked momentarily confused. "You're not here for a potion, are you?"

"Afraid not," the sheriff said. "We've got a few questions about your recent dating habits."

I glanced at Sheriff Nash. "This doesn't make sense. Florian doesn't date witches."

"Well, he went out with me," she replied, with a roll of her violet eyes. "He said he only did it to make his mother happy."

"He told you that?" I queried. It didn't seem typical of Florian. He seemed perfectly happy to bypass his mother's wishes.

She gave me a pointed look. "Why do you think there was only one date?"

"And what about Cayden Mercer?" I asked.

"Cayden?" She glanced from me to the sheriff. "Oh. I get it now. Is this about Frogmaggedon?"

I stifled a laugh. "Good one."

Bryony blew out a breath. "I guess you would need to question me. I went out with Thom Rutledge, too, but you probably already know that."

"We do," the sheriff said. "I spoke to someone at the Wishing Well, who said you two were together the night before his transformation."

Her brow lifted. "He was found as a frog the next morning?"

"He was," the sheriff said. "So you can understand why we'd like to hear more about these dates. Think of us as interested girlfriends."

"Forget it," Bryony said. "I'm only giving you the minimum level of detail required by law. You can't make me say anything else."

Sheriff Nash straightened. "Sounds like a challenge, Miss Pennywhistle."

"You'd like that, wouldn't you?" Bryony suggested slyly. "Being a werewolf and all." She groaned. "I'm swearing off werewolves, though. I can't keep falling for the same type of guy over and over again. I hate to agree with my mother, but it isn't healthy."

"The date with Cayden didn't go well?" I asked.

"He spent most of our date tracking the waitress with his

eyes," Bryony said. "Admittedly, her boobs were amazing, so I could understand it, but still..." She blew a strand of pink hair out of her eye. "No girl wants to be with a guy when his roving eye is in full force. It's humiliating. And my rack is nice to look at, isn't it, Sheriff?" She puffed out her more than acceptable chest.

I watched with amusement as the sheriff struggled to respond in an appropriate way. "It's perfectly in proportion with the rest of your body."

Bryony shot me a triumphant look, as though I'd disagreed.

"Did you say anything to Cayden?" I couldn't imagine biting my tongue in a situation where my date's attention was so clearly on someone else.

She examined a violet fingernail that matched her eyes. "I may have used a little magic on his fried chicken."

My brow lifted. "Magic that turned him into a frog?"

Bryony held out her wrists. "Sure. Arrest me now." She burst into laughter. "Of course not. Suffice it to say, he likely spent the night embracing his toilet."

I wrinkled my nose at the thought.

"And Thom Rutledge?" the sheriff asked.

"The incubus?" She smiled dreamily. "We met in the Wishing Well. Danced to the live music. What was the band called?" She snapped her fingers. "Hocus Pocus."

The sheriff's face lit up. "They're really good." He elbowed me again. "That's the kind of band you should go and listen to, Rose."

"I'll make a note of it." I turned my attention back to Bryony. "Did you leave the Wishing Well with Thom?" I remembered that the incubus had been discovered as a frog in bed.

"Had to. I lost a bet."

That piqued my interest. "What was the bet?"

Bryony chuckled. "Let's just say there were a lot of body shots involved and I overestimated my abilities."

"And after the shots?" the sheriff asked.

"A lady never kisses and tells, but I will say that he was well fed." She paused and another smile touched her lips. "A midnight snack *and* breakfast."

"What time did you leave?" the sheriff asked.

Bryony looked thoughtful. "Early. I had to be here to open the store and get the fresh batch of potions ready. My part-timer only works in the afternoons and she's not trained as a mixologist."

"And how did Thom seem when you left?" the sheriff asked.

"Asleep," Bryony said. "The heavy snoring was a big clue. He was *very* tired." She winked at the sheriff and he shifted uncomfortably.

"You didn't notice anything unusual?" I asked. "Did you see anyone else when you left his place?"

Bryony shook her pale pink head. "I thought I heard a neighbor's door when I left. Otherwise, it was just the birds in the trees, serenading me during my walk of shame." She didn't appear to be remotely shameful, which was perfectly fine with me. What two consenting paranormals got up to was their own business, as far as I was concerned.

"I'll just ask you this one time," the sheriff said. "Did you give these men any potions or use any spells that would turn them into frogs?"

"Absolutely not," she said. "In fact, I was disappointed to hear about Thom. I was hoping to have another...meal with him soon."

"Hopefully, you will," I said. "We're determined to get to the bottom of this. Aren't we, Sheriff?"

He gave me an amused look. "Of course we are, Miss Marple."

"Miss Marple?" I echoed. "Wasn't she an elderly spinster?"

He grinned. "See? The resemblance is uncanny."

Bryony reached for a bottle on the counter. "I have something you might be interested in, Ember. Come back another time and we'll talk about it." She flashed an innocent smile at the sheriff. "Let me know if you need anything else from me, Sheriff."

"Because you're such a team player?" he queried.

"I am when it comes to matters that impact me directly," she said. "And Thom Rutledge as a frog definitely impacts me directly. Small and green doesn't really do it for me."

"Kermit will be so disappointed," I said.

Bryony gave me a blank look.

"What? We know Miss Marple here, but not Kermit?" I was outraged on behalf of The Muppets. "Forget it. Let's go, Sheriff. I need to get back to the office and see if Bentley has followed up any of his leads. We have our own bet going."

The sheriff appeared alarmed. "You do?"

I waved him off. "Not like Bryony's bet." Popcorn balls, no. "It's for a byline."

"Look at you," the sheriff said, as we left the store together. "Using fancy journalist vocabulary. They might make a reporter out of you yet, Rose."

"I'm pretty sure that's the idea." Now if only I could drum up enough information on the case, I might actually get to report on it. With Bryony out of the running, though, my chances were getting slimmer by the minute.

CHAPTER 11

"Mom, are you sure that's what you want to wear tonight?" Marley asked.

I glanced down at my blue T-shirt and capris. "What's wrong with this?"

"Nothing, if you're going to the grocery store," Marley said. "You're supposed to be going on a date. I think he might expect a little more effort."

I shrugged. "What? I'm wearing lipstick. Anyway, it's not a date. A new friend is showing me around town."

Marley groaned. "Whatever. Why did you even agree to go out with him?"

"Because he seems like a nice elf," I said. "And maybe I feel secretly guilty for not making an effort to provide you with a male role model."

Marley made one of her sassy faces. "Don't pin this on me. I just don't want you to waste your youth. If you wait until I'm a grown-up to date, who knows what shape you'll be in by then?"

"Gee, thanks," I said. "Nothing like a vote of no confidence from my daughter."

"Change your clothes the old-fashioned way," Marley insisted. "But you need to learn to do spells like our cousins. They could create something awesome with the snap of their fingers."

I had to admit, that was a pretty nifty trick. I had a feeling it would take me a while to reach that level of sophistication.

"I have an idea," Marley said. "Why don't we ask Aunt Hyacinth to magic you an outfit?"

I barked a short laugh. "So I can show up in a hot pink kaftan? I thought you wanted me to look good tonight."

Marley laughed. "You have a point. Okay, go back and look in your closet. Didn't Linnea choose a dress for you from the Pointy Hat? You should wear that."

"But then it looks like I'm interested in him," I said.

Marley cocked her head. "But he already thinks it's a date, doesn't he?"

I shrugged. "I don't see why he should. It wasn't presented that way."

"You should still wear the dress," she said. "It's nice to look your best. Besides, you never know. You may actually like him. He's cute, right?"

"He's an elf," I said. "Of course he's cute. It's stamped into their DNA."

I marched to my bedroom and retrieved the dress from my closet. By the time I'd slipped the dress over my head, I heard a knock at the door. Well, at least he was punctual. That was already a point in his favor.

"I'll be right there," I called. From upstairs, I heard PP3's growl reverberate through the cottage. Not again. He'd been so territorial since our move to Starry Hollow. Not that I should be surprised. The whole experience had been an upheaval for all three of us. PP3 chose to cope by treating most visitors like suspected terrorists.

I came downstairs to see Ben seated on the couch in the

115

living room. Marley stood in the kitchen doorway, with a struggling PP3 in her arms.

"He won't settle," Marley said.

"That's okay," I said. "Ben and I are headed straight out anyway, aren't we?"

He stood and smiled at me. "Whatever you wish. You look lovely, by the way. That's a very pretty dress."

Behind him, I saw Marley smirk.

"Thank you," I said. "I like your...bowtie." It reminded me of the bowties Aster's four-year-old sons had worn the first time I'd met them. Ben was already in the cute category. The bowtie only served to keep him there.

We left the cottage and I immediately noticed his car—a yellow convertible. While I liked convertibles in theory, the reality was that the blast of air turned my hair into Spanish moss. I'd need an industrial-strength hairbrush to get the knots out by the time we arrived at our destination.

Ben sensed my hesitation. "Is there a problem?"

"I hate to be a spoilsport," I began, "but is there any way we can ride with the top up?"

He flashed me a look of surprise. "You don't want to take advantage of the convertible?"

"I don't have the luxury of thick hair like my Rose-Muldoon cousins." The simple truth was that my hair was thin, although I had a lot of it. That translated into a serious case of flyaway hair whenever the slightest breeze came along.

He looked so disappointed, I felt sorry for him. "It's no problem. The top goes up with the push of a button. I just assumed that you'd like the top down. Most girls do."

"Most girls with luxurious manes." Unfortunately, I didn't fall into that category.

As we drove into town, Ben took the time to mention places in passing. He showed me several art galleries, Willow

Park, and a row of colorful houses called the Painted Pixies before he pulled into the parking lot of Elixir.

"I hope you like cocktails," he said. "This place is famous for them."

"I've been wanting to come here," I said. "Marley and I pass it on our walk to and from school. And I know Florian likes it here."

"It's a pretty cool place," he said. "Especially coming from the human world. You won't have seen anything like it, I suspect."

I couldn't imagine what would be so different about a cocktail bar in a paranormal town, but I was willing to keep an open mind. The moment we stepped through the door, I understood.

"Great popcorn balls of fire," I said.

"Pretty sweet, huh?"

He wasn't kidding. The place was amazing. Everywhere I looked, my eyes were met with bottles of glowing liquid. They were suspended from the ceiling, attached to the walls, even built into the flooring beneath our feet. It was like standing in the middle of a giant lava lamp.

"It's disorienting," I said, trying to maintain my balance.

"You'll get used to it," he said with a smile. "Do you want to look at a drinks menu or would you like me to choose the first round?"

"I actually think I'll let you," I said. It was unlike me, but I felt like I could stand there all night and not make a decision. The list was sure to be overwhelming—far more intense than the coffee options at the Caffeinated Cauldron.

"There's a table over there," he said, pointing. "Go ahead and sit down and I'll get us drinks."

I nodded and threaded my way through the crush of bodies to reach the available table. It was definitely a popular choice for a night out. I sat alone at the small table, drinking in the scene. I noticed fairies chatting with elves and some guy that looked like an enormous bull but wore human clothes. Weird. Marley would know what he was, not that I'd bring her to a place like this simply to act as a reference guide.

Because the place was crowded, it didn't surprise me that Ben took a while at the bar. As I surveyed the room, a crisp linen suit stepped into my line of sight and I glanced up into the chiseled face of my boss.

"Good evening, Miss Rose," he said. "What a surprise. Are you drinking alone this evening?"

I inclined my head toward the bar. "No, I'm here with a new friend."

His brow lifted almost imperceptibly. "And who, might I ask, is the lucky gentleman?"

"Well, I don't know how lucky he is," I said. "He's certainly not getting lucky tonight, not with me anyway."

Alec stared at me. "You don't need to explain yourself to me, Miss Rose. What you do outside of work is your business."

"His name is Ben Witherspoon," I told him. "He owns Snips-n-Clips."

Alec nodded. "Yes, I'm familiar with the place, although I have my grooming done elsewhere."

Of course he did. Alec Hale was far too polished for Snips-n-Clips.

"It isn't polite to keep a lady waiting this long," Alec said. "What would you like to drink?"

"You don't have to do that," I said. "Ben's in that crowd somewhere. I'm sure he's having a hard time getting the bartender's attention." A nice guy like Ben could end up waiting a long time. He probably let all the women cut in front of him. He seemed like that kind of guy.

"Have you ever had a Breezeburst?" Alec asked. "I have a

feeling it's something you would enjoy."

"Everything sounds good in Starry Hollow," I said. "Makes it difficult to choose."

Without another word, he disappeared into the crowd. I already knew he was stealthy—what I didn't realize was how quickly he moved. He was back in less than a minute, holding a drink in each hand. He set a colorful glass in front of me.

"My treat," he said.

I studied the bright liquid. It reminded me of layers of Jell-O. The red, green, and orange stripes of the drink were bright and cheerful. I hoped they tasted as good as they looked. I took a hesitant sip.

"Sweet baby Elvis," I said, my taste buds luxuriating in the afterglow. "That's the most amazing thing I've ever put in my mouth."

Alec smiled softly. "I thought you might like it." He took a sip of his own drink. Some kind of martini. Very masculine yet refined.

At that moment, Ben emerged from the crowd, holding two glasses. He'd clearly had the same thought as Alec because one was a Breezeburst. When he saw the glass in my hand, his face fell. His gaze darted to Alec and his shoulders slumped in defeat. I felt awash with guilt for accepting the drink from Alec. I should have waited.

"Ben," I called cheerfully. "Come and sit down. Your legs are probably tired from all the standing around the bar."

Reluctantly, he joined me at the table and gave Alec a nod.

"Ben Witherspoon, this is my boss, Alec Hale."

Ben offered his hand. "I know who you are. I'm a huge fan of your work."

"You read the paper?" I asked. "You didn't mention that."

"I do read the paper, albeit not regularly," Ben said. "But that's not the work I mean."

I glanced from Ben to Alec. "What does he mean?"

Ben gaped at me. "You don't know?"

I took a long sip of my cocktail. Dear angels in heaven, it truly was incredible. "I really don't know. Will someone please tell me?"

"Mr. Hale is a writer," Ben said.

I shook my head in confusion. "Yes, I know. He's the editor-in-chief of the paper."

"No, you don't understand," Ben said. "A novelist. He writes books. He's very well known in the paranormal world."

I scrutinized Alec. "You write books? What kind of books?"

"Books that people like to read, apparently," Ben said. "He's a bestseller. I would love it if you'd sign my copies. I have a whole collection at home."

I was gobsmacked. Alec shifted uncomfortably.

"If you bring them by the office one day this week, I would be more than happy to sign them for you," Alec said in a clipped tone. He didn't sound particularly enthusiastic. Not that Alec sounded enthusiastic about anything. He had that whole vampire 'been there, sucked that' attitude.

I finished my first drink and Ben slid a second one across the table to me. "You might not want to drink those too fast. They'll hit you hard."

"If there's one thing I'm good at, it's handling my liquor," I said.

"Well, I'll let you two get acquainted," Alec said. "I didn't mean to intrude."

"You're not intruding," I said. "Pull up a chair. Ben doesn't mind. He's just showing me one of the coolest places in town. Right, Ben?" My head suddenly began to spin. Ben was right. The drink was having more of an effect than I realized.

Ben begrudgingly pulled over a chair. "The more, the merrier."

An attractive woman with long, dark hair rested her hand on Alec's arm. "There you are, Alec. I wondered where you wandered off to. Come back to the table. Portia is telling the most hilarious story about her trip to Elf Haven."

"In a moment," Alec said, gently removing her hand from his arm. He looked at me with such intensity, my entire body tingled. "Enjoy your evening, Miss Rose."

"Thanks for the drink," I said, and squelched a burp before I completely embarrassed myself.

I watched as he disappeared into the crowd with the dark-haired woman. I wondered whether she was his girl-friend. He hadn't mentioned anyone special in the office. Then again, he didn't often discuss personal matters.

Ben snapped his fingers in front of my face. "Ember, are you listening?"

I squeezed my eyes closed and opened them again. "Sorry. Must be the drink."

"Why does he call you Miss Rose if he's your boss and you call him Alec?" Ben asked.

The cocktails had loosened my lips. "My daughter thinks it's because he's making an effort to keep me at arm's length. If he doesn't use my first name, then he's managing to maintain distance from me."

"I guess he doesn't like to befriend his employees," Ben mused. "It's tough to be a boss like that. Not that I would know. My relationship with Robina is as personal as it is professional."

"Tell me more about that," I said. "You mentioned at your shop that she's like a mother to you. How did you two meet?"

"She'd just moved to town," Ben said. "I own an apartment building, and she became one of my tenants. We became friendly because I live on the top floor and we'd bump into each other all the time. She told me later that she worried I wouldn't rent to her because of her criminal history."

I took another sip of my drink. "But you rented to her anyway?"

Ben nodded. "Everyone deserves a second chance," he said. "She served her time. There was no need to punish her further. I felt it was my civic duty to help get her started on the path to rehabilitation."

"That's very noble of you," I said.

"More selfish than noble, really," he said. "She had this motherly quality from the moment we met. I really warmed to her. And she makes a mean cup of tea."

"Would you mind if I ask what her crime was? The sheriff said it was serious, but no one said what it was."

"She used fairy magic to divert funds from senior citizens in Blue Moon Valley," Ben revealed.

"That's horrible," I said. Robina seemed like such a nice woman. I couldn't imagine her doing something so awful to innocent people. Then again, it was hard to really and truly know someone's character. It was always on the news—neighbors and family members expressing disbelief over the actions of a person they thought they knew well.

"She's very sorry for what she did," Ben said. "I know she wishes she could take it all back. She's not that fairy anymore."

"I guess not, without her wings," I said. I clamped my hand over my mouth. "Sorry, that was a little rude."

"She's still a fairy at heart," Ben said. "You can take her wings and her wand, but the fairy still lives inside her."

"So they took her wand away, too?" I asked. "Can't she just get another one?"

Ben shook his head. "She's on a 'no wand' list. If she goes into any wand shop in a paranormal town, her name will come up as someone who's banned from practicing magic."

"Is that why she had to have her fairy friend help with the magic in the shop?"

Ben nodded mutely.

"Wow," I breathed. "That's hardcore."

"The paranormal world takes magical crimes very seriously," Ben said.

"What about the kind of magic that's turning bachelors into frogs?" I asked. "Is that a serious crime?"

Ben appeared thoughtful. "I don't know about serious, but it's definitely a crime."

I thought of poor Florian, trapped inside an amphibian's body. I wondered whether he was uncomfortable, wherever he was.

"What are you thinking about?" Ben asked.

I gave a quick shake of my head. "Just taking it all in. This new life is pretty weird, if I'm being honest." I suddenly became acutely aware of my full bladder. "Can you point me to the restroom?"

Ben gestured to the back of the bar. "There's an alcove back there with both restrooms."

"No finishing my drink while I'm gone," I said, wagging a finger at him. I was definitely buzzed.

"I'm happy to get you another one while you're gone," Ben said. "Unless you'd like to try something else."

"I think if I have another one of anything, you'll end up carrying me out over your shoulder," I said. "That's probably not what you want."

He chuckled. "My upper body strength isn't what it should be." He flexed a puny muscle. "Elf genes, you see. Not much I can do about those."

I smiled. "I'll be back as quickly as I can."

I maneuvered my way through the crowd to the alcove, bumping into a few bodies along the way and muttering apologies. Alec emerged from the men's room just as I entered the alcove.

"How about that?" I said. "It didn't occur to me that vampires would need to pee."

He gave me an amused look. "We drink and eat," he said. "The waste needs to go somewhere."

"I guess if you can make babies, then you can urinate," I said, and my cheeks burned. That alcohol was hitting me hard. I needed to stop talking.

Alec moved closer to me. "Apologies. What's this about making babies?" His voice was soft and inviting. I hoped I was able to shield my thoughts successfully while drunk. I had a feeling I was doing a poor job of it.

"You're doing fine," he said, his breath warm on the curve of my neck. "And might I add, you look particularly lovely tonight. You should wear that dress to the office."

I looked up and gazed into his green eyes. They were absolutely mesmerizing. "When will you call me Ember?"

"Why? Do you dislike being called Miss Rose? I like to think it's respectful."

My heart beat rapidly inside my chest. His lips were only inches from mine.

"A rose by any other name smells as sweet," I said. "But I guess you know that, being a secret author and all."

He grinned. "I'm not a *secret* author. Simply because you don't know something doesn't make it a secret."

"I want to read something of yours," I said, and pressed my palms flat against his chest. "I want to glimpse your soul." Then I laughed. "Wait a minute. You don't have a soul, silly. You're a vampire."

In the dim light, I saw the points of his fangs appear. "I am. And you should not forget it." He gripped my hands and gently pushed them away, although I realized that he had not let go. We were still holding hands when Ben appeared in the alcove.

"I only came to check on you," he said, his gaze flitting

from Alec to me. "I was worried that you were too drunk to find your way back."

"She is fully conscious, as you can see," Alec said, stepping back. "I'll leave you to your evening."

He disappeared before I could say anything else. I slipped into the bathroom to pee and felt guilty for making Ben wait in the alcove. When I emerged from the bathroom, he was slouched against the wall, his gaze pinned to the floor.

"It's hard to compete with a guy like that," he said. "His suit costs more than my mortgage."

"First, you're acting as a new friend and showing me around," I said. "There's no competition. Second, Alec's my boss. There's no way I'm getting involved with him. This job is a big opportunity for me and I wouldn't want to do anything to jeopardize it."

Ben remained sullen. "But he's so perfect. He could have any woman in this bar." He paused. "He probably has."

"I don't know about that," I said. "He's not much of a player from what I've seen. He keeps to himself."

Ben smiled. "Except when he comes to Elixir."

"I guess so. To be honest, I'm also a little afraid of him," I admitted. "I know you must be used to vampires, but I'm still adjusting to the idea. I see his fangs every time he looks at me."

"Is that so?" Ben asked.

"Of course," I said. "Like I said, he's a vampire."

Ben gave me a funny look. "Just so you know, you don't always see a vampire's fangs."

"No, you don't. It probably depends on their teeth and the shape of their mouth."

Ben laughed, his sullen mood lifted. "Okay, let's go with that." He slipped an arm across my shoulders. "Come on, Miss Rose. You've had enough to drink. Let me take you home."

CHAPTER 12

I STOOD at the bottom of the steps of the marble building, admiring the six enormous columns at the front. A statue of a witch stood atop the roof, holding a moon skyward.

"Are you excited for your first coven meeting?" Aster asked. She'd driven me to the Silver Moon headquarters after Mrs. Babcock, Thornhold's resident brownie, arrived to look after Marley.

"This place looks more intimidating than I expected," I said. I'd only seen it from the air when Marley and I had taken the broomstick tour of the town.

Aster patted my arm. "It'll be fine. Let's go in. Mother likes us to be punctual. It sets an example for the rest of the coven."

We walked up the steps together and walked through the portico entrance doors. A man stopped us inside.

"I need to check your bag, miss," he said. He stuck out his wand and touched the outside of my bag. "All clear, thank you."

I shot a brief glance at Aster. "Security?"

"Dillon is the Watchman," Aster said. "He handles safety

and security for the coven, among other things. Dillon Stanton-Summer, I'd like you to meet my cousin, Ember Rose. This is her first coven meeting."

"Welcome to the Silver Moon coven," Dillon said. He was an attractive wizard with light brown hair, a square jaw, and plenty of muscles.

"Thank you," I replied.

Dillon gave Aster a quick peck on the cheek. "You look beautiful, as always. Where's my cousin?"

Aster sighed. "Sterling will be here. He's running late. You know how he is with work."

"He needs to slow down and enjoy life a little more," Dillon said. "He'll work himself into an early grave."

"I wouldn't object if you told him that directly," Aster said. She flashed an encouraging smile.

Dillon offered a sympathetic look before focusing on me. "If you ever need a protective ward or some other type of magical protection, that's what I'm here for."

"Is security really an issue for the coven?" I asked. "I mean, what did you think you'd find in my bag?"

Dillon fixed his hazel eyes on me. "Your cousin Florian is currently living out his days as a frog."

I twitched at the mention of Florian. Marley and I still hadn't told anyone that Florian was quite possibly living out his amphibious life in the woods behind the estate.

"Imagine if whoever cast that spell did it during a coven meeting," Dillon continued. "You'd have an entire room full of frogs. It would be anarchy."

"But whoever cast the spell on Florian wasn't in the dining room with us, or with the other two guys when they became frogs. How would you have prevented that?" I was genuinely curious.

"If we know there's the potential for harm, we can arrange a protective spell," Dillon said, his square jaw set and serious. "But we can't prevent every attack. It simply isn't possible."

Aster clapped the Watchman on the shoulder. "You do an excellent job for the coven, Dillon. No one's suggesting otherwise."

"I really wasn't," I added. "I'm new. I've got no clue how things work." And should probably keep my big mouth shut.

Aster looped her arm through mine. "Come along, Ember. Let's mingle before the meeting. This is a good time for a chat with other members of the coven."

A thin elderly man approached us. Unfortunately, his balding head was right at my eye level, which left me no choice but to stare at the strands of gray hair that swept across the top of his shiny dome.

"Excuse me, Miss Rose," he said in his gravelly voice, "but there's the matter of your dues to discuss."

I blinked. "My dues?"

"Argyle Pennywhistle is the Pursewarden," Aster said.

The last name sounded familiar. "Are you related to Bryony Pennywhistle?" I asked.

"My granddaughter," he said. "She's the best mixologist in the coven. Owns a cute little store in town called Charmed, I'm Sure."

"Yes, I've been there," I said. I didn't feel the need to mention why. Argyle probably didn't want to know his granddaughter had been hot and heavy with an incubus.

"It would be nice to have the best mixologist in the coven attend a meeting on occasion," Aster said. The reprimand was loud and clear, although I felt sorry for Argyle. It wasn't his fault if Bryony chose not to come.

"I wholeheartedly agree," Argyle said. He peered at me. "Now, young lady, about your dues…"

"Speak to Mother," Aster interjected. "She'll take care of it."

"Very well, then," he replied with a slight bow. He caught sight of someone behind me and his face paled. "Mind your backs, witches, Camille is headed this way."

He scurried off before the dreaded Camille reached us.

"Who's Camille?" I asked, but there was no time for a response.

"Why, hello, my lovely new sister." Camille's loud voice reverberated throughout the room. Even worse, it had that annoying singsong quality. Where was Dillon and his protective spell when I needed him?

"Camille, I'd like you to meet my cousin, Ember Rose." Aster turned to me. "Ember, this is the coven Bard, Camille Poppywick."

"Bard?" I asked. "Like Shakespeare?"

"I'm the musical director," Camille said, practically bursting into song. With her large body, ample bosom, and blond braids sticking out from behind her ears, she reminded me of the cartoon version of an opera singer. Stick a Viking helmet on her head and she'd be perfectly cast.

I inclined my head. "The coven performs musicals?"

"Once a year," Camille replied. "My main responsibilities are to keep our original songs and ballads alive. I also lead the coven in chants or songs during rituals."

"Camille also provides accompaniment on a variety of instruments," Aster said. "She's the boys' piano teacher."

"And they are progressing *very* nicely, my dear," Camille said. "Not that I'm a bit surprised. The Roses are chock full of talent, after all." Camille examined me. "You seem like you might be good at something. How's your singing voice?"

"You'd have to ask my shower," I said. "The acoustics in there are excellent, though, so probably not an accurate assessment."

"Showers always are," Camille agreed. "I'd love to have you involved. I'm always on the hunt for musical volunteers."

"Always," Aster said with a tight smile.

The sound of ringing bells sent everyone scurrying to the next room. I followed Aster inside the cavernous hall and tried to keep my jaw from hitting the floor. The hall was incredible. The only light came from the hundreds of candles set up along the perimeter of the room and from three candlelit chandeliers above. There were three enormous wooden tables in the middle of the hall, about twenty feet long and five feet wide. At the front of the room was a single, smaller table that faced the hall. I recognized the witches and wizards seated there because I'd met them during my induction ceremony. The High Priestess, the High Priest, the Summoner, the Crone, the Mother, and the Maiden. On the end of the table sat Gardenia, the Scribe. Her iPhone was already on the table in front of her, ready for copious note-taking. My gaze zeroed in on the Summoner. He was as creepy now as he was the night of my ceremony. Beside him rested his signature blackthorn staff.

Aster guided me to seats toward the front. Linnea was already there with Aunt Hyacinth. I cringed when I noticed the empty seat beside her—probably Florian's. My aunt gave me a slight nod as I slipped into my chair.

I glanced across the table and saw Hazel and Marigold huddled next to each other. They were probably comparing notes to see in which class I sucked more. My money was on runecraft.

I felt dozens of pairs of eyes on me, which was understandable, since I was an oddity. A new witch in town from the human world with no knowledge of her powers. Definite weirdo.

Another bell rang and the room quieted. Iris Sandstone, the High Priestess, stood in her silver cloak. The Silver Moon crown on her head glistened in the candlelit room.

She raised her arms in the shape of a V. "O' wondrous Goddess of the Moon. Let us give thanks."

A gust of wind blew through the hall and the flames flickered. I got goosebumps on my arms, ready to experience a majorly atmospheric meeting—until the Scribe stood to speak.

"The monthly Silver Moon coven meeting is now called to order," she said, and proceeded to summarize the minutes from the previous meeting. "And now the Pursewarden will give us the financial report."

Argyle stood from his place at the middle table. "The homemade candle fundraiser made a net profit of $1,200," he reported. "That leaves enough money in the budget for new robes for the incoming class."

"Class?" I whispered to Aster.

"The eleven-year-olds who come into their magic," Aster replied in a hushed tone.

I surveyed the room but saw no sign of small people. "Why aren't there any kids here?"

"The children don't start attending coven meetings until they turn eighteen," she whispered.

Aunt Hyacinth gave us both a look that would have wilted a cactus. I straightened in my chair and resolved to save all my questions for the end.

The rest of the meeting was uneventful. It was like attending a PTA meeting, not that I was ever able to participate in many of those, between my work schedule and single parenthood. Most school events were designed around a two-parent household.

After the Crone announced changes to her individual counseling schedule, the High Priestess stood and opened the floor to new business.

Aunt Hyacinth pushed back her chair without waiting to

be acknowledged. Everyone turned to her with rapt attention.

"Good evening, my lovely coven. First, I'd like to take a moment to welcome my niece, Ember Rose, to her first official coven meeting."

A smattering of applause greeted me and I found myself smiling so hard that my cheeks began to ache.

"As many of you know, Ember left Starry Hollow as an infant and was raised in the human world. We're taking great care to slowly introduce her to the world of magic. For those instructors who haven't yet heard from me, rest assured that you will."

Across the room, a hand shot up. Aunt Hyacinth nodded crisply.

"You don't think incantations should be higher on the priority list?" a deep male voice asked.

Aunt Hyacinth bristled. "Are you questioning my approach, Wren?"

"You know I'm not as bold as that," Wren said, and I heard a few snickers in the crowd. "I haven't had the pleasure of teaching a Rose. I'm looking forward to the challenge...I mean, the opportunity."

"I'll bear that in mind," Aunt Hyacinth replied. "Anyone else want to throw a hat in the ring to be next on the schedule? How about you, Lee?" She directed her attention to a dark-haired man next to Hazel. "Surely we can all agree that the rigors of ritual toolcraft are a priority for a new witch. By all means, let's have her bedazzle a chalice."

No one spoke.

"On to other matters," Aunt Hyacinth said smoothly. "I'm sure you're all wondering about the status of my afflicted son."

There were murmurs of interest around me.

"You'll be pleased to know that Sheriff Nash is working diligently to apprehend the magic user."

My ears perked up. Aunt Hyacinth was speaking well of the sheriff? When did that change occur?

"I've also requested that the staff of my newspaper investigate the matter," she continued. "That way, no stone is left unturned."

"Are there any leads?" Iris asked in her soft-spoken voice.

"There have been a few and more information comes to light each day," Aunt Hyacinth said. "I have complete faith that my son will be restored to me in perfect health very soon." She paused. "And the other gentlemen, too, of course."

"Thank you for the update, Hyacinth," Iris said. "We're all hopeful that the matter is resolved quickly."

I leaned over to Aster. "Since when does she think the sheriff does a good job?"

"This is her public face," Aster whispered. "You'll learn soon enough."

She had a public face? That meant I couldn't take her words at face value. Popcorn balls. I was from New Jersey. We only had one face for all occasions—pissed off.

Iris ended the meeting with a request to donate used wands to the Empty Cauldron, an organization for needy witches and wizards. Aster had forgotten to mention this one in her list of charities.

We filed out of the hall and were met by trays upon trays of baked goods and a table of colorful, sparkling drinks. Linnea scooped up two star-shaped cookies and handed one to me.

"You have to try this one," she said. "It's my favorite."

"I didn't realize there'd be treats at the end," I said. "I would've come last month." No one laughed.

"Why do you think the meetings are so well attended?" Aster queried. "Everyone's waiting for the best bit."

I bit into the star cookie. Although it didn't look like anything special, the taste was off-the-charts incredible. It was like a canon fired chocolate and salted caramel straight into my mouth. I stared at the cookie.

"This doesn't even look like it has chocolate or caramel in it," I said. "How can it taste like this?"

"Those must be your favorites," Linnea said.

I frowned. "They are."

She smiled and finished off her cookie. "Mine tastes like chocolate and mint."

"It's called a Wishing Star," Aster explained. "It tastes like your two favorite flavors."

"But they all look the same," I said. "How is that possible?" Inwardly, I berated myself for such a dumb question. *How was it possible?* How was any of this possible? Magic, of course.

"I serve these to guests sometimes," Linnea said. "But I don't do it often because I can't seem to stop myself from having one too many." She cast a sly glance at Aster. "Sort of like Aster and alcohol."

"Take that back, Linnea," her younger sister said, indignant. "I do not overindulge in anything."

"Yes, that's what Sterling says," Linnea shot back.

My eyes bulged. This was the first time I'd heard the sisters bicker and, I had to admit, I found it fascinating.

To my dismay, Aunt Hyacinth's sudden presence stopped the bickering in its tracks. "My driver is out front. Ember, why don't you ride with me? That way Aster can go straight home to Sterling and the boys."

"Sterling never made it to the meeting," I said.

"No, he texted me," Aster said. "He got held up at work and went straight home."

I knew he was the president of Hexed Brewing Company, a business that manufactured various magical alcoholic drinks. He kept the Rose-Muldoon family well stocked with their favorite brands.

I polished off my cookie and tried not to moan out loud. It was *that* good. "Ready when you are, Aunt Hyacinth."

As we maneuvered through the throng of coven members toward the exit, a handsome wizard stepped between us and the door. He was tall and muscled with a square jaw, not unlike the Watchman.

"What is it, Wren?" Aunt Hyacinth asked coolly.

"Sorry about earlier, ma'am," he said. "You know I didn't mean anything by it. Just having a little fun." He flashed a charming smile and I was surprised to see Aunt Hyacinth actually relax her stern expression.

"Yes, Wren. You're always trying to have a little fun," she replied. "Something you and Florian have in common. I'm surprised you're not hopping around town right now."

"Florian and I tend to drink from different wells, if you know what I mean."

Aunt Hyacinth patted his cheek. "Yes, at least you tend to limit your philandering behavior to witches. My son could learn a thing or two from you."

Wren appeared amused. "You think so?"

"Of course, darling. It's a numbers game. The more witches he dates, the more likely he is to fall in love with one of them."

"Then how do you explain my continued bachelorhood?"

"Stubbornness," Aunt Hyacinth replied. "Speaking of stubborn, have you met my niece, Ember?"

Wren stuck out a hand. "I've been hoping for an introduction. Wren Stanton-Summer."

"Dillon's brother?" I asked.

"We're fraternal twins," he replied. "A rarity among wizards."

"Wren is the Master-of-Incantation," Aunt Hyacinth said. "You'll be working with him...eventually."

So, I'd been saddled with a crazed clown and a cheerleading drill sergeant when I could've been working one-on-one with this magical piece of prime wizard beef? I suddenly felt deprived.

"I'm always up for new lessons," I said. "Bring on the incantations."

"You'll have a chance soon enough," Aunt Hyacinth said. "It was good to see you, Wren," Aunt Hyacinth practically dragged me out the door.

The car was waiting directly in the front of the building. I slid into the backseat beside her, thinking how pleasant it would've been to stay behind and talk to Wren. He certainly seemed eager to talk to me. That wasn't going to happen as long as I was being carted around by family members.

"Aunt Hyacinth," I said slowly.

"I agree, my darling," she said, and gentle patted my thigh. "I think it's time you have your own car."

CHAPTER 13

I PUSHED OPEN the door to the newspaper office, a cup of coffee with a shot of fizzle in my hand. The barista had assured me I'd love it, so I decided to give it a whirl. If I expected Marley to try new things, then I had to lead by example.

"Must be nice to get mornings off," Bentley said, typing away on his keyboard.

"I don't get them *off*," I shot back. "I have witch training, unless you'd prefer I practice here on you. I'm getting very good at throwing objects around a room with my mind." Okay, maybe a slight exaggeration.

"Dig up any new leads on FrogGate?" he asked, ignoring my comment.

"Wow, a Watergate reference in Starry Hollow? Someone's educated on human history." I plopped down in the chair next to him.

"I have a keen interest in political news, human or otherwise," Bentley said. "You would, too, if you were a real journalist."

Tanya fluttered over, ready to separate the two of us if the argument got out of hand. I didn't envy her job.

"Where's our fearless leader?" I asked. "I want to update him on my part of the story." In actual fact, I hadn't seen him since the other night at Elixir and wanted to make sure I hadn't said or done anything stupid. I distinctly remembered locking eyes with him near the restroom, but that was the extent of it.

Bentley looked intrigued. "You have something to report?"

I gave him a haughty look. "Not to you."

Bentley scowled and returned to his screen.

"You might not want to disturb him now," Tanya said. "He hasn't come out of his office for hours."

"Are you sure he's even in there?" I asked. The vampire was stealthy enough that he easily could have left the office without anyone realizing it.

"Now that you mention it, I'm not sure," Tanya said. "I've been in and out myself. Had to fly over to the healer's office to get my right wing checked. It's been aching when I wake up in the morning."

"Is everything okay?" I asked.

"Lyssa thinks I may have pulled a muscle where the wing connects to my back." Tanya brightened. "That reminds me…"

"No, no," Bentley said. "I told you I'd take care of it."

I looked from Bentley to Tanya. "Take care of what?"

Tanya shot the elf a disapproving look. "Now, Bentley, I'll not play favorites." She faced me. "While I was in the waiting area, I heard a pixie mention that Lyssa went out with Florian only two weeks ago."

"I don't remember her name on the list," I said.

"It wasn't," Bentley confirmed. "So maybe there's a reason."

"How about that? Someone slipped through Simon's net," I mused. "We should go talk to her now."

"I was just preparing my questions," Bentley said.

"Let me poke my head in to see Alec and then we'll go," I said. I wasn't giving Bentley a chance to leave me behind. I strode to the back of the office and gave his door a gentle knock. No response.

"Alec?" I leaned closer to the door and pressed my ear against it. "Alec, are you awake?" I didn't bother to ask if he was alive since I already knew he was undead.

Still quiet. I decided to risk a reprimand and pushed open the door. There was no sign of Alec. Just a tidy desk with a small laptop, a neatly aligned stack of papers, and a few books. Then I spotted his phone on the floor.

"That's odd," I said. As I crouched down to pick up the phone, something jumped out at me and I screamed. It took me a moment to pull myself together and realize there was a green frog hopping beside me.

I squinted at the frog. "Alec?" The frog seemed irate. Tiny frog fangs poked out of his mouth and I knew for certain.

As much as I hated to touch the slimy creature, I cupped the frog in my hands and prayed it didn't pee on me.

"Tanya," I yelled. "I think you're going to want to come in here."

She yelped upon entering the office. "Great sparkles! Is that...?"

"I'm afraid so."

Bentley joined the fairy in the doorway of Alec's office. "He still has fangs."

"Weird, right?" I set Alec the Frog on the desk. "We need to contain him until the sheriff arrives." I didn't want him disappearing in the middle of town. That would be much worse than the pond in the woods.

Tanya whipped out her fairy wand. "I can help with that."

She scrunched her nose as she focused on the frog. "Super duper, frog-in-stupor."

The frog appeared to freeze on command, his eyes large and unblinking, as though he was too confused to move.

"That's pretty good," I said.

Tanya gave me a bashful smile. "Fairies and frogs are like witches and broomsticks."

I scratched my head. "You can fly on frogs?" Seemed a bit pointless when the fairies had wings.

"No, silly goose. I mean that we learn how to do frog spells early on. It's part of the basic curriculum."

"Why frogs and not—I don't know—puppies?"

Tanya tucked away her wand and pulled out her phone. "I don't make the rules, dearie. Now let me get the sheriff over here before the spell wears off."

Sheriff Nash arrived within ten minutes, a look of pure pleasure on his unshaven face.

"I don't think you're supposed to look happy about this," I pointed out.

The sheriff quickly adjusted his features to reflect concern. "Who's happy? These are my citizens being turned into frogs. Do you think I wear this gold star because it goes with my outfit?" He tapped the sheriff's star pinned on his shirt.

"I hope not because it completely clashes."

He glared at me. "No one saw anything?"

"No," Tanya said. "He seemed fine this morning when he came in."

The sheriff walked around Alec's office, examining the surroundings. He stopped to poke through the pile of books on the desk. "He sure has written a lot of books."

My expression shifted to surprise. "Oh. These are *his* books?" I'd been meaning to grab one to read. I studied the first three titles—*Glorious Soldier, Journey to B'zen, The Final Prophecy.*

"Which one would you recommend?" I asked.

The sheriff chuckled. "You think I've read any of them? I don't read fantasy. I like more grounded stories."

Fancy that. The werewolf sheriff preferred stories based in reality. What a world I lived in now.

"*The Final Prophecy* is his most popular," Tanya said. "And it features a kick-butt heroine with a flaming sword."

I whipped toward her. "Seriously?" I couldn't imagine Alec writing about a kick-butt anything.

"I enjoyed it," Tanya added. "It's a very clean read."

I picked up the book and began to leaf through the pages. "Clean? Like no swearing?"

"And no s-e-x," she whispered.

"Well, that's a disappointment." I tucked the book under my arm. "But I'll read it anyway."

"That might be evidence," the sheriff said.

My brow creased. "You just don't want me to read it."

Sheriff Nash appeared horrified by the suggestion. "Do you think I would use the investigation to prevent you from reading a book you can easily borrow from the library?"

"Yes," Tanya and I answered in unison.

The sheriff shook his unruly head. "Now that's downright insulting."

"Still taking the book," I said.

"Whatever. You take the book and I'll take Alec down to the station to join his friends."

That gave me pause. I knew that Alec wouldn't like being trapped in the sheriff's office even in frog form, not with their hostile relationship.

"Um, how about I take the frog, too?" I said.

The sheriff eyed me suspiciously. "You want to take home the book *and* the frog?"

"Why not?" I asked. "It would only mean more work for you to keep him at the station. One more frog to monitor and feed."

"They're not difficult to feed," the sheriff replied.

"Perfect," I said. "Anyway, Marley has always wanted a frog for a pet. This is her chance to test the pond waters."

"Is it really wise to keep him in your house?" Sheriff Nash asked.

"What do you think is going to happen? The frog's going to jump on me in the middle of the night and suck my blood?"

The sheriff shrugged. "I wouldn't put it past him."

Tanya huffed. "Alec Hale would do nothing of the sort. Frog or not, you know perfectly well what a gentleman he is. If Ember wants to keep him comfortable in his current state, I don't see why anyone should object." Her passionate reaction seemed to surprise the sheriff.

"Fine," he said. "Just don't lose him. I don't need a vampire frog on the loose. It's bad enough that we have another frog at all."

That was true. If word got out, people were going to start demanding action.

"I'll tell you what," Bentley said, appearing in the doorway. "If you agree to share all your information with us, Sheriff, we'll agree not to tell anyone about the most recent enchantment."

Since the sheriff was already sharing information with me anyway, it wasn't much of a deal, but Bentley didn't seem to realize that.

The sheriff grinned. "You strike a hard bargain, Bentley Smith."

Bentley wore a smug expression. "I almost went into law, but decided on journalism at the last minute."

I rolled my eyes. Bentley didn't even realize when he'd been had.

"Good move, not telling the sheriff about Lyssa," Bentley said.

We'd stopped by the cottage to drop off Alec the Frog before heading to the healer's office. On the way, Bentley informed me that Lyssa McTavish was an assistant healer who worked alongside Cephas, one of the druid healers in town.

As we approached the entrance, Bentley leaned over and said, "Now, let me handle the bulk of the questions. From what I know, she's a fairy with an eye for the lads, so she'll be more receptive to questions from me."

"I believe you'll find she has an eye for the extremely good-looking lads," I said pointedly. "Not sure you'll get much more than a firm handshake."

As we approached the reception desk, the squat man behind the window smiled in greeting. A dwarf. He slid the window aside. "Are you here for an appointment?"

"No," Bentley said. "We work for *Vox Populi* and we'd like to speak with Lyssa. Is she available?"

The dwarf frowned. "I'm afraid she's busy with patients at the moment. She finishes work at six. I'm sure she'll have time to speak with you then."

"I think you must have misheard me," Bentley said. "I'm the associate editor for *the* weekly paper in Starry Hollow. Perhaps you're a reader?"

I could tell by the dwarf's face that Bentley wasn't going to get anywhere with his approach. I gently shoved him aside.

"Hi there," I said. "My name is Ember Rose. My aunt owns

the paper my esteemed colleague mentioned. Perhaps you've heard of Hyacinth Rose-Muldoon?"

The dwarf examined me. "You're one of them, are you?"

"I am," I replied, folding my arms expectantly.

"Then why is your hair so dark? Shouldn't it be white-blond, like all those other Roses?"

"I favor my mother," I said. "Or so I'm told."

The dwarf set a clipboard up on the counter with blank forms. "The only way to see Lyssa McTavish during hours is if you're here as a patient."

Bentley and I exchanged looks.

"You're new in town," Bentley told me. "I bet you need a physical for something."

I grabbed the clipboard off the counter. "Okay, fine. I'll do it." I scribbled in the information as quickly as I could. At least I had the necessary passport that allowed me access to medical care in town. The passport was basically the all-access pass to Starry Hollow.

Bentley and I spent the next fifteen minutes in the waiting area arguing about whether the plural of dwarf should be dwarves or dwarfs. Thankfully, the glass was thick enough that the single dwarf behind it couldn't hear us. By the time my name was called, I was ready to abandon Bentley in the waiting area, but he was a persistent elf and insisted on accompanying me.

We sat in the exam room snooping around for any evidence of fairy foul play. Although I doubted very much that she'd leave anything obvious at the office, it was worth a look.

Lyssa finally swept into the room, her purple wings sticking out of her white lab coat. I imagined there was a whole cottage industry for fairy clothing that accommodated wings.

"Hello, I'm Lyssa McTavish, the assistant healer to

Cephas. It says here that you're a new patient, Miss Rose." She stopped and stared at the form. "Rose? Are you related to Florian?"

"He's my cousin," I said. I waited to see whether she would reference his current amphibious state.

"A shame about what happened," Lyssa said. "It's all my patients can talk about."

"I'm sure people are on edge," I said. "Nobody wants to be the next victim."

Lyssa laughed. "I have a hard time thinking of Florian as a victim, even in frog form."

Bentley titled his head. "Why is that?"

"Because he's Florian Rose-Muldoon," she replied. "His flies are probably fed to him on a silver spoon."

"Do you know Florian?" I asked.

"More than I'd like to," she said. "He's been my patient here a few times, and pestered me to go out with him every time he came in. I think he may have even faked an illness to get an appointment with me."

Bentley and I exchanged glances.

"Imagine that," I said. "Someone faking a need for an appointment to talk to you."

"Crazy, right?" She laughed. "So, I finally relented."

"You went out with him?" I asked.

"About two weeks ago. He wanted to have dinner, but I said drinks only." She hesitated. "I always insist on drinks for a first date. It's awful to suffer through a whole meal if you realize you don't like your date."

"Did you like Florian?" I queried.

"Hard not to, really," Lyssa said. "He's charming, hot, wealthy, and available. He ticks every box."

"But?" I prompted.

"I felt like I was nothing more than a challenge to him," she said. "Once he got me to go out with him, he seemed to shift into autopilot. He was very persuasive when he was coming by the office. In the bar, though, he struck me as…lazy."

Lazy. Yep, that pretty much summed up my cousin.

"Were you annoyed?" Bentley asked. "Maybe annoyed enough to turn him into a frog?"

Lyssa laughed. "I use my fairy magic to heal, not to harm, Mr.…?"

"Smith," he finished for her.

"And if I did want to get back at Florian," she continued, "I'd certainly show more imagination than a frog curse from Fairy Spells for Beginners."

"There's also a protection spell to keep other magic users from turning him back into a wizard," Bentley pointed out.

Lyssa shrugged. "Still remedial magic, as far as I'm concerned. I think I mastered both of those spells when I was a child."

Show-off. "So how did you leave things with Florian?" I asked.

"I had one drink in the time he had two," she said. "I went home straight from the bar. He didn't seem interested in seeing me again, which was fine, because the feeling was mutual."

Out of the corner of my eye, I noticed Bentley type something on his phone. Notes. He and Gardenia had something in common.

"And you're here for a physical?" Lyssa said to me. "Is this a requirement by your employer?"

"It is," Bentley said. "I should know. I'm her employer."

I gave him a sharp look, even though I really wanted to give him a sharp jab with my elbow.

Lyssa fixed her attention on him. "Is it typical for you to accompany your employees to their physicals, Mr. Smith?"

"It's not typical, but Miss Rose hails from the human

146

world and we're keen to make sure that she doesn't bring in any contagions to her new place of employment."

Lyssa appeared skeptical. "What kind of contagions are you particularly concerned with?"

Bentley struggled to come up with an answer. "The kind you find in New Jersey."

Lyssa snapped her fingers. "Right, you've lived in the human world your whole life, haven't you?"

I nodded. "I didn't even know I was a witch until recently. I'm still catching up."

She whistled. "That's a lot of catching up."

"My aunt is trying to introduce magic slowly," I said.

"That's smart," Lyssa agreed. "You don't want to over-whelm your system. It's a good thing you came in for a physical. Now we have a baseline to work from as your magic gets more advanced. We'll be able to monitor you for signs of stress."

"No need to monitor me," I said. "Signs of stress are whole bags of Doritos and chocolate. Very easy to spot."

She laughed again. "Why don't you put on this gown and we'll get started?"

I shot a pained look at Bentley. I had to actually go through with the physical?

"You heard Miss McTavish," Bentley said, barely disguising his smirk. "It's a good thing you came in."

"Mr. Smith," Lyssa beckoned, "why don't we give her privacy while she gets changed?"

They left the exam room and I stared at the gown on my lap. The lengths I went to for a story...I guess I was becoming a real journalist, after all.

CHAPTER 14

THE FIRST THING Marley spotted after school was the new addition to the cottage. Alec the Frog sat in a portable dog crate that I'd bought for PP3.

"Did you find Florian?" Marley asked, rushing to press her face against the side of the crate.

"Not yet. This is Alec."

Marley stared at me. "Uh oh. Not another one. You're keeping your boss in the dog carrier?"

"What choice do I have? He's a vampire frog. Check out his tiny fangs."

At the mention of 'tiny fangs,' the frog's tongue lashed out and smacked the side of the crate before he sucked it back in.

"I think I insulted him," I said, suppressing a laugh.

"I don't think they can understand us in their frog forms," Marley said. "Otherwise, Florian would've come back instead of hopping away at the pond."

PP3 began to sniff around the base of the crate. Although he disliked riding in it, he seemed annoyed to see it occupied by another animal. When the barking began, I knew it was time to move the frog to safety. I picked up the crate and headed for the stairs. The last thing I needed was to find my boss's green legs hanging out of my Yorkie's mouth.

"Where are you taking him? Marley asked.

"Away from our vicious beast," I replied. "I'm not in the mood to see a frog drawn and quartered by a dog."

Marley laughed. "PP3 can't open the crate. He's not a velociraptor."

"Better safe than sorry," I called over my shoulder. I set the crate on the dresser in my bedroom. "There you go, boss. Nice and comfortable until this whole thing blows over."

Marley appeared in the doorway. "Mom, can we go check for Florian again before I do my homework? I'm not going to be able to concentrate."

Her statement gave me pause. Marley never got distracted enough to delay homework.

"Okay," I said. "Let me get changed out of my dress first. With my luck, I'd fall in the water and get pond scum all over my nice work clothes."

"I'll get the pond net," Marley said, her eyes shining with excitement. We'd picked up a pond net on the way home from school after much pleading and blinking of big, blue eyes. Cuteness was her superpower.

She disappeared downstairs while I peeled off my dress and pulled shorts and a T-shirt from the drawer. My bra and underpants were a little bit sweaty, but it didn't make sense to change them before chasing a frog around the pond. I changed my shoes and blew the vampire frog a kiss before joining Marley downstairs.

"Should we leave PP3 behind?" Marley asked.

"I think that would be best," I replied. "If Florian *is* there, we don't want to scare him off."

"Sorry, Prescott," she said, giving the dog a pat on the head before we left the cottage.

Marley babbled happily as we left the grounds of the estate and headed into the woods.

"This is my favorite kind of tree," Marley said. She swung on a low, crooked branch like it was a monkey bar.

"It's called a live oak," I said. "We don't have them in New Jersey."

Marley glanced upward. "Some of them are so big."

"Probably because they're very old." I stared at the large tree. "My dad used to talk about live oaks. He thought the trees in New Jersey were puny in comparison."

"I thought he never talked about Starry Hollow," Marley said, now using the pond net to scoop up acorns off the ground.

"He never mentioned the town specifically, but he definitely talked about live oaks. I remember because he said the wood from live oak was difficult to work with, but very strong, like me." I smiled at the memory. "I guess I can see what he means."

"Do you miss your dad?" Marley asked. "You never talk about him."

I blinked back tears. "Every day."

Marley picked up an acorn and chucked it into the brush. "I miss mine, too."

I reached for her and kissed the top of her head. "At least we have each other."

"I wish you'd known your mom. I bet she was awesome, like you."

"No way," I said. "I bet she was way more awesome than me. Like Wonder Woman awesome."

Marley beamed and took my hand. "You're Athena awesome."

"The one that was born out of the god's head?"

She laughed. "Zeus. You never remember his name."

I tapped my chin. "So, you're calling me the equivalent of a giant headache."

"No," Marley said in protest. "She's the goddess of wisdom. She's the best one."

"What? There's no goddess of Dorito eating?" Now that was a field I could dominate.

Marley gasped. "I see frogs." She ran ahead to the pond, clutching the pond net.

"You can't catch them all," I said. "They're not Pokémon. And what if none of them is Florian? Either way, we'll have all these frogs in the house after the spell is broken." Assuming the spell could be broken. I thought of Artemis Haverford's boyfriend and shivered. It seemed there were no guarantees when it came to magic.

Marley stood at the edge of the pond and observed the two frogs on lily pads. "Do you think one looks more like Florian than the other?"

I scrutinized the frogs. "Not really. They're both small and green. I don't see any telltale markers, like Alec's fangs."

"What do you think would happen if we let Alec loose out here?" Marley asked. "Would he bite the other frogs?"

"No clue." And not eager to find out.

"Here, froggy," Marley called and whistled to the frogs.

"What's the point of calling them both?" I queried. "You only want the frog that's Florian. Not to mention the fact that Florian might be the frog we put back in the enclosure at Thornhold." The uncertainty was driving me bonkers.

Marley lunged forward, trying to scoop one of the frogs into the net. It quickly hopped out of reach.

"Couldn't we use magic to decide which frog was Florian?" she asked. "Even if we can't turn him back ourselves?"

I shook my head. "That's above my pay grade, sweetheart. And if we ask for help with a spell, then we'll have to admit what we did."

Marley bit her lip. "I don't love our options."

"That's why they're called hard choices." I contemplated the frogs. "Let's do this. Spend the next ten minutes trying to catch one or both. If we don't manage it, we'll go home and try again another time. You have homework to do and I need to make dinner."

"I hate the idea of leaving him here again," she complained.

"But we don't know that we are," I said. I gave her shoulder a squeeze. "Try to have faith, Marley. The frogs seem to like this pond, so if he is out here, we'll find him when the time comes."

Marley hefted the pond net. "Ten minutes?"

I set the timer on my phone. "Ready. Set. Go."

Marley ran around the pond, careful not to fall into the water. She reached and splashed with the net to no avail. The frogs outsmarted her by staying smack dab in the middle of the pond, just out of reach. The timer beeped, signaling an end to Capture the Frog.

"One more minute," Marley pleaded.

"A deal's a deal," I said. "Let's go. Duty calls."

"What do you think Aunt Hyacinth would do to us if she knew what happened?" Marley asked.

I glanced over my shoulder at the frogs in the pond. "Probably turn us into flies."

Marley shuddered. "Let's never tell her. Promise?"

Good to know her instinct for self-preservation was firmly intact.

"Promise."

Just as I told Sheriff Nash I would, I returned to Haverford House with cleaning supplies, a makeup bag, and my champion helper, Marley. Unsurprisingly, she'd insisted on coming along under the guise of 'seeing' Jefferson for herself, but I knew that her real plan was to stick to me like glue. I'd given her the whole story about Artemis Haverford and Jefferson, thinking that she'd be too scared to join me. It seemed to have the opposite effect.

"This is the perfect chance to practice your telekinetic skills," Marley said. "And whatever you can't do with magic, I'll be there to help you."

"It's not going to be an easy task," I said. "Even the dust has dust."

"All the more reason I should come. I'm a much better cleaner than you."

Aunt Hyacinth's driver was kind enough to deliver us to Haverford House, prompting my aunt to mention my need for a car again. Although I'd managed walking into town and to school, places like Haverford House were too far to go on foot. A car would also make grocery shopping easier. So far, I'd been using a backpack and buying only as much as I could carry.

Artemis was so shocked by our arrival, she appeared to be suffering from a case of the vapors. I half expected her to shout for her smelling salts.

"Good afternoon, Artemis," I said. "You said I was welcome back anytime, so here I am. And I brought my daughter, Marley."

Emotion flooded the old witch's face. "You brought a child...to see me?"

I brushed past her and into the darkened house. "I guess I can see why that's not typical."

Marley stuck out her hand. "Nice to meet you, Miss Haverford."

The witch looked from Marley to me in disbelief. "Based on the mop in your hand, I gather you're here for an altogether different purpose than matchmaking."

"In the human world, we have all these TV shows revolving around makeovers," I said. "There are more than a dozen house shows where a decrepit place is transformed into a grand home and plenty of shows about transforming people." Whether it was weight loss or choosing more flattering clothes, there seemed to be a show for every kind of transformation.

"And that's what you plan to do here?" she queried. "A makeover?"

I held up a shopping bag. "On your house *and* you."

She gestured for us to come further into the house. "You know, Miss Rose, there are many people in town that would think you're downright crazy to insult me like this. Haven't you heard? I'm a scary old witch."

I blinked. "Insult you? This is the highest compliment. Do you think I take time out of my busy schedule to help just anybody?"

Marley gave a solemn shake of her head. "Trust me. She doesn't. She's not a people pleaser."

Artemis appeared mildly amused. "So what is it about me that made you decide I was worth the trouble?"

I studied her. "You lost someone you loved and you've locked yourself away ever since. Let's say I can relate to that."

"Your husband?" Artemis asked.

"Daddy died four years ago in an accident," Marley interjected. "I keep trying to get Mom to start dating again, but she's resistant."

Artemis pursed her pruned lips. "Resistant, is she?"

"Busy more than resistant," I said.

"I have many successful pairings under my belt," Artemis said. "I take great pride in my work."

"I'm sure," I said. "But I'm still adjusting to a new life in a new town as a descendant of the witch to beat all witches."

Artemis chuckled. "The One True Witch."

"That's the one." I sighed. "I don't feel capable of putting my trust in someone new right now, not while I'm navigating this insane path."

"Without trust, my sweet, there is no hope for a relationship," Artemis said.

I folded my arms. "You see my dilemma."

"You had fun with Ben," Marley interjected.

"Having fun with someone isn't the same as wanting a romantic relationship with him," I said. And, to be honest, I'd preferred talking to Alec, a realization that refused to die a quick death. The thought was like the vampire himself, stealthy and popping up when I least expected it.

"It's a good start, though, isn't it?" Artemis said.

I ignored her remark. I had zero romantic interest in Ben cute-as-a-button Witherspoon and no one could convince me otherwise.

"I think we should start down here," I said, surveying the main floor. This would definitely be a multiple-day job.

"I'll have Jefferson bring us some tea first," Artemis said. "Give us our strength. And what about for you, young lady? A glass of milk?"

"If you throw a little chocolate in there, I'm sure that will do the trick," I said.

Artemis smiled. "That can be arranged."

I'd warned Marley about the witch's rotting teeth before our arrival. I hadn't wanted her to react to the gruesome sight. To her credit, Marley's face remained expressionless.

Marley couldn't hide her pleasure when the tray floated into the room and a tall glass of chocolate milk found its way into her eager hand.

"Thank you, Jefferson," Marley said, glancing awkwardly around the room.

"He's over by the hutch," Artemis said, with a flick of her bony fingers.

Marley focused her attention on the hutch. "Thank you," she said again.

"Artemis can't see him," I said. "But she can sense him. Not just his location, but his emotions, too, isn't that right?"

She nodded. "Our connection has grown stronger over time. It took me many years to develop such a keen sense of him. He and Clementine are my only company most days, unless I have a customer."

At the mention of her name, Clementine ambled into the room. I imagined her as a kitten at one time, tearing through the house and clinging to the heavy drapes by her claws. Marley, of course, wasn't the least bit bothered by the sorry state of the cat. She approached her with the same excitement as she would a beautiful Abyssinian kitten.

"Hi, Clementine," she said. "Look at you, pretty girl."

Clementine approached her cautiously, sniffing the air around her. I watched nervously as Clementine lowered her head, allowing Marley to touch her.

"Well, that's a huge endorsement," Artemis said. "You are most certainly welcome here, young lady. Clementine isn't a moody cat, but she is very particular."

Marley beamed.

"Marley has always had a special way with cats," I said. "Except Fanta. It took years for Marley to win her over."

"That was our neighbor's cat," Marley explained. "She finally let me pet her without biting me, and then we ended up having to escape to here the same day."

Artemis shot me a quizzical look. "What does she mean by that? Why did you have to escape to here?"

I relayed our story about Jimmy the Lighter and the Rose-Muldoon cousins coming to save us.

"And I thought my story was interesting," Artemis said, folding her arms. "Color me impressed."

After tea, we set to work, pulling down the heavy drapes

and replacing them with sheer curtains to let in the sunlight. Marley dusted every item within reach.

I used Linnea's old wand to perform basic cleaning tasks. Grow my magic muscle. I watched with satisfaction as a mop moved back and forth across the wooden floors. I only managed to finish the foyer before I felt myself losing energy. That was less ground than I'd hoped to cover.

"Why doesn't Jefferson clean?" Marley asked, as she dusted between the spindles of the banister.

"That's not his role," Artemis said. "And I haven't been bothered enough by the mess to do anything about it."

"Because you've been too busy wallowing in self-pity?" I asked.

Her eyes popped. "My, my. You are direct, aren't you?"

I shrugged. "Listen, nobody does you any favors by pretending your living quarters are acceptable. People must be desperate to come here for matchmaking, given the state of the place." *And the state of you*, I thought.

Artemis inhaled deeply and focused on the mop. "I'm not telekinetic, but I used to know a good many spells for moving objects." She twisted her index and middle fingers and muttered a phrase I didn't recognize. The mop began to glide across the floor again.

"Great," I said. "You should probably do the living room next. The foyer's pretty much done."

The mop floated through the room until it reached its destination.

"What else is on your list?" Artemis asked.

"You." I held up my cosmetics bag. "Where's your bedroom? I need to see what else is in your closet besides that tattered dress you insist on wearing. I'm no historian, but I'm pretty sure it went out of fashion in the 1850s."

Artemis suppressed a smile. "Upstairs. First door on the right."

"You hang out here with Marley and I'll see what I can find." I took the stairs two at a time and was surprised to see Clementine keeping pace with me. She was probably concerned I was moving in on her territory.

The master bedroom looked like something out of Southern Belle Magazine, if such a thing existed. The room smelled musty and stale, and I choked back a cough. I was assaulted by frills and lace in every direction. Standing in the room was like hiding under a hoop skirt.

Before I could reach the closet door, an unseen hand opened it for me.

"Um, thanks," I said. Although I couldn't see Jefferson, I had to assume he was responsible.

An apricot-colored dress floated out of the closet. "That's your choice, huh? It looks good as new."

I watched as the dress floated to the bed. The floor-length dress was tasteful and pretty for a woman of any age. I wondered how old it actually was.

"She's thin as a beanpole, so I guess it will still fit," I mused.

From the down the hallway, I heard the sound of running water. I followed the noise until I reached a grand bathroom with a candlelit chandelier and a deep, clawfoot tub. The water was slowly rising in the tub and I realized what Jefferson was doing.

"Good idea, but I draw the line at bathing her," I said. "Feel free to lend a transparent hand. Make sure you wash behind her ears."

A bottle of scented body wash floated down from the shelf. It appeared full and unopened. Maybe a thoughtful gift from a grateful customer.

"I'll let her know you've drawn her bath," I said, exiting the bathroom.

What an old witch and a ghostly manservant got up to in the privacy of their own bathroom was their business.

When I returned downstairs, Marley and Artemis were playing a game on the coffee table.

I gave Marley a pointed look. "You've abandoned your chores already?"

"It was time for a rest," Artemis said. "No need to accomplish everything in one visit."

Very wily, old witch. She wanted a reason for us to come back.

"Is this chess?" I asked, observing the board.

Marley grinned from ear to ear. "It's a special coven chessboard."

"It belonged to my father," Artemis said. "Marley was kind enough to dust off the pieces."

The board itself looked normal enough, but the chess pieces were different from the ones I'd seen in the human world. The figures were witches, wizards, elves, dragons, and some fat guys that may have been trolls. The game was like the love child of Dungeons & Dragons and chess.

"They move across the board for you," Marley said. "You just tell them where to go and they do it."

"Amazing," I said. "Imagine if children were as obedient as these chess pieces."

Marley stuck out her tongue. "You're lucky and you know it."

"Jefferson is running your bath," I said. "And there's a clean dress on your bed."

Artemis looked at me in disbelief. "You were serious about the makeover, weren't you?"

"As serious as a vampire's fangs," I replied. If that wasn't already an expression here, I was making it one.

"Mom brought a cosmetics bag, too," Marley said.

"There's a new toothbrush and toothpaste in there. Bubble gum flavor."

"Bubble gum flavor," Artemis repeated. "Well, I do declare. I shall have to try that."

"It's my favorite," Marley said.

Clementine appeared at the foot of the chair, mewing at Artemis.

"It seems my bath is ready," Artemis said. "Miss Marley, can we continue this game another time?"

Marley looked at me for approval and I nodded.

"Yes, please," Marley replied.

"I'll have Jefferson keep the board intact," Artemis said, rising to her feet.

"You keep the cosmetics bag and experiment with the colors," I said. "Choose whatever you like."

"I will," she said. "Thank you, my sweet."

"See you later, Miss Haverford," Marley said with a cheerful wave.

I plucked my phone from my pocket and called the driver to come and get us. We gathered our cleaning supplies and headed for the door.

"Thanks for letting me come, Mom," Marley said. "I had a lot of fun."

Only my child would express enjoyment over a visit to an old witch's haunted house where she dusted furniture and played chess. She was weird, but she was mine.

"Come back soon," Artemis called. "Next time we'll tackle the kitchen."

Sweet baby Elvis. The kitchen was probably a disaster zone. I glanced at Marley and sighed.

"We're going to need a bigger mop."

CHAPTER 15

IN ASTER'S perfectly managed schedule, the ideal time to introduce me to the Wish Market fell between one o'clock and three o'clock on Friday. As long as I was finished before the middle school day ended, it suited me fine. Naturally, Bentley gave me the stink eye when Aster turned up at the office to drag me away.

"Just because the boss is a frog doesn't mean you're free to do as you like," he said under his breath. He wasn't foolish enough to be overheard by Aster.

"She wants to show me the Wish Market," I said. "I haven't been."

"It is impressive," he admitted.

"What do you care?" I asked. "The less I'm here working, the more likely you are to win the bet."

Bentley rubbed his chin. "I hadn't thought of it that way." His narrow face brightened. "Go on, Ember. What are you waiting for? All sorts of goodies at the market."

I followed Aster out the door and we walked the two blocks over to where the outdoor market was located.

The Wish Market defied belief. The walls of the outdoor

market stretched as high as the eye could see. It almost seemed like an optical illusion. Wicker baskets were stacked at the entrance and Aster plucked one off the pile and handed it to me.

"You'll definitely be needing one of these," she said.

"I don't know where to look first," I said.

My eyes darted from the jars of exotic spices to the lanterns to the brass hospitality stars that adorned many of the gates around town. Food, textiles, hats, trinkets. Anything you could imagine seemed to be available within the confines of the market.

"Take your time," Aster said. "It's easy to get overwhelmed."

"Why is it called the Wish Market?" I asked. "Because everything you could possibly wish for is here?"

"Not quite," she replied. "If you see something you like, you wish for it in your mind and it appears in your basket. Take that hat, for example." She pointed to a wide-brimmed sunhat high above us on a floating pedestal. "If I decide I want it, I simply picture it in my basket and voila."

I glanced down to see the hat in my wicker basket. "Sweet baby...what is it you guys say here? Stars and rocks?"

"Stars and stones," Aster said with a smile. She was incredibly beautiful, but even more so when she flashed those pearly whites.

"Stars and stones," I repeated. "I just walk around and look? What if I accidentally picture something in my basket that I shouldn't have?"

"Returns are simple," she said. "You picture it back where it came from."

"Is that a boogie board?" I asked, pointing to a stall to the left. One of my favorite childhood memories was crashing through the waves on the Jersey shore with my flamingo-covered boogie board. My father had loved the beach, probably because it had reminded him of home.

"Not just any boogie board," Aster replied.

I studied the green board featuring a large silhouette of a black cat. "Let me guess. A magic one?"

She shrugged. "What else?"

"What does it do?"

"Buy one and see for yourself."

"Marley would love it," I said. "How can I get it to fit in my basket?"

"Easy as an incubus," Aster said. "Just wish it smaller in your mind. Then when you get it home, wish it back to its usual size."

"The wishing will work once it's out of the market?"

"Yes, because you bought it here. Or you can simply wish it back to your cottage. That way you don't need to carry it if you don't want to."

My brow creased. "Doesn't that encourage stealing?"

"Not here," Aster said. "The market knows when and how an item leaves the premises. You'll be charged before you leave the market's border."

"Very cool, and yet kinda creepy," I said.

Aster nodded toward the board. "Go ahead and try it."

I pictured the boogie board in my head and then imagined it appearing in the living room of the cottage. I leaned it against the side of the sofa.

"Done?" Aster asked.

"I think so," I said, and then noticed that the boogie board in the market was gone. "Okay, I guess I know so."

"Anything else you'd like? Something for the cottage?"

"Not for my place, but I'd like something for Artemis."

Aster balked. "Artemis Haverford? Whatever for?"

"I'm pretty sure she hasn't updated her decor since the Civil War," I said. "The house needs a touch of something modern." I wasn't a big shopper, but even I recognized the need to spruce up your environment once in a century or two.

"Well, if we head down this lane, we can browse home interiors." She hesitated. "You might not want to mention to Mother that you're taking an interest in Artemis."

"Why not?" What could Aunt Hyacinth possibly have against the elderly matchmaker?

Aster remained vague. "Trust me, Ember. Mother won't approve."

"The list of things your mother approves of is short and sweet, isn't it?"

"It's all about standards, darling," Aster said, in a perfect imitation of her mother.

After a few rows of crystal and brass hospitality stars, I spotted a sundial for the wall with the image of a cat in the middle.

"That one," I said, gesturing to the wall.

"That?" Aster wrinkled her nose. "Are you sure?"

"Don't worry, Aster. It's not for you." I couldn't imagine an item like the cat sundial as part of Aster's white Pottery Barn-style decor.

She looked relieved. "If you think Artemis would like it…"

"I do."

She shrugged. "Then wish it wherever you'd like it to go."

"Can I send it directly to her house?"

"You can," Aster said. "Imagine it with a note from you."

"Seriously?" Take that, UPS. I closed my eyes and imagined a note to Artemis, along with the sundial. When I opened my eyes, the sundial on the wall was gone.

Aster linked her arm through mine. "You're getting the hang of this, cousin. You shop like a true Rose."

"I should probably get going," I said. "I need to pick up Marley from school. If the weather stays nice, maybe I'll take her to the beach to try out her new present." *Her new present*. I couldn't remember the last time I bought Marley a present for no reason. Probably never. How our lives had changed so drastically in such a short time. Holy crap, I was grateful.

"The weather will stay nice," Aster said. "This is Starry Hollow, after all."

Marley and I strolled down to Balefire Beach so that she could try out the new magical boogie board. I had no idea what to expect, but I was pleased that Marley was willing to try something new. Then again, what ten-year-old wouldn't want to try out a boogie board?

"How fast do you think it goes?" she asked. She stood at the water's edge, clutching the top end of the board.

"Apparently, as fast as you want it to go," I said. "So don't go overboard."

Marley groaned. "Mom joke alert."

"That one was unintentional."

I set up my beach chair and umbrella and settled down to watch Marley embrace her inner daredevil. She dipped a careful toe into the water before deciding it was warm enough and calm enough to proceed. The sand was smooth and soft, without the numerous broken shells and seaweed that populated Jersey beaches.

"The water's so clear," she called over her shoulder.

"Go ahead," I encouraged her. "I want to see that magic board in action." I cracked open *The Final Prophecy* and began to read.

I only made it through the first few pages when a shadow passed over me. "I see you managed to get your hands on one of his books."

I shielded my eyes from the sun and peered up at Ben. "Hey there. Fancy meeting you here."

"This is one of my favorite spots," he said, dropping down in the sand beside me. "It's never very crowded."

"I'm so used to being around a lot of people," I said. "In apartments, in cars, in stores. Moving here is like being on a permanent vacation."

"Except you need to work and continue your same responsibilities," he said.

I shrugged. "Trust me. I'm busy, but it's a good busy. Even though I'm still wrapping my head around this whole new life, it's still a hundred times better than where I was."

I clapped loudly as Marley grabbed her first wave. The board skimmed the top and inched slowly toward the shore. Even the roll of the wave seemed to slow in order to accommodate her comfort level.

"She's cautious, huh?" Ben said.

"She's very safety conscious," I said. "She'll gain confidence the more times she does it."

I watched as the board did a U-turn and carried Marley straight back out to catch the next wave. She didn't need to do anything but stay on. Her smile was so big, I could count all her teeth from my beach chair.

"I think she's enjoying it," Ben said.

"That's all I need to be happy," I said, and heaved a sigh of contentment. I'd take all the craziness Starry Hollow had to throw at me if it meant a safe and happy child.

"There's a lot more she can do with that," Ben said. "Would you like me to show her?"

"That's nice of you, but I'd rather let her move at her own pace," I said. "She'll resist if she senses someone is pushing her to move forward before she's ready."

"Stubborn, huh?"

I smiled at him. "Runs in the family." I opened a bottle of water and took a long sip. "What brings you here at this hour? Shouldn't you be at your shop?"

"This tends to be the quiet time of day. Robina keeps an eye on things when I want to escape for a bit."

"Did you hear about Alec?" I asked.

Ben cocked his head, which somehow accentuated the pointy tip of his elven ear. "What about him?"

"He's joined the bachelor frog brigade."

His kind eyes rounded. "You're kidding. Alec Hale? Someone's either very brave or very stupid."

"I'm keeping him safe at my cottage," I said.

"That's sweet of you," Ben said.

"Wow. I don't think anyone's ever called me 'sweet' before." Unless you counted the construction workers that called me 'sweet cheeks' and 'sweet meat.'

Ben chuckled. "You don't fool me. That tough chick thing is your persona. The real you is quite sweet."

I cast a sidelong glance at him. "I think you've been drinking magical Kool-Aid. I don't even hold doors for people. Not on purpose, though. I just don't even think about it until the door is partially closing and then they have to catch it before it bashes them in the teeth."

"That's not tough," he said. "That's just inconsiderate."

We laughed. "I'm trying to be better, for Marley's sake. She deserves a kinder, gentler parent. She doesn't have a father to balance me out."

Ben looked thoughtful for a moment. "Did you manage to speak with Artemis Haverford? Maybe that's why Alec was targeted? If she thinks he sent you to do a story."

I dusted sand from my shins. "It's not Artemis. I can see why we needed to question her, but she's completely innocent."

"How do you know?"

"Because I do. I've even been back to see her since then."

He choked back a laugh. "Seriously? She didn't put the fear of the gods into you?"

"The whole place was super creepy," I admitted. "But it's looking better now. And she's out of that hideous white doily she pretended was a dress."

Ben gaped at me. "You...fixed her up?"

"Not completely," I said. "Her teeth need more help than I can give. I'm not a professional, for Pete's sake. And there's still plenty of work to do on the house, too, but it's a good start. At least the heavy drapes and dust are gone. It was high time that pale skin got licked by the sun again."

"I don't even know what to say." He shook his head. "Why did you feel compelled to go back?"

I'd asked myself the same question. "Because one day I might be a scary old witch living alone and I might secretly want someone to come by and tell me that I matter by changing me out of my butt-ugly clothes and having my ghost manservant run me a bubble bath." I took another sip of water. "See? Not sweet at all. I did it for purely selfish reasons."

"Yeah, totally selfish."

"You should talk, anyway," I said. "You're the one who decided to appoint a former criminal as your mother figure and business partner. Talk about sweet."

He inhaled the salty sea air. "I honestly don't know where I'd be now if it weren't for Robina. Her magic changed my life."

"You mean her friend's magic," I said.

Ben blinked. "Yes, of course. It was Robina's ideas that we implemented, though. She was the mastermind."

Mastermind. Interesting choice of words to describe a criminal.

We turned our attention back to the ocean, where Marley was gliding across the water at a slightly increased speed. Her hair was blown back by the breeze and her smile was as wide as the stretch of beach. Observing her now, I felt the stirrings of maternal pride.

Ben gave me a shy look. "Ember, would you like to go out again soon?"

Did I want to? Not for romantic reasons, but I didn't object to the idea of a new friend.

"I wouldn't mind seeing more of the town that's off the beaten track," I said. "I'm helping Aster on the tourism board and I'd like to highlight some of the more interesting aspects of the town. She seems determined to emphasize every grain of sand on the beach instead of elements that might actually interest tourists."

"I can definitely help with that," he said. "How about later tonight? Eight o'clock? My apartment building is smack dab in the middle of town, so it's the perfect starting point. If you take the elevator to the penthouse, I have the whole top floor of the building. It's not the view from the Lighthouse, of course, but it's nice."

He gave me the address.

"Great," I said. "Sounds like a plan."

CHAPTER 16

I SAT on the edge of my bed, completely absorbed in *The Final Prophecy*. I peered over the top of the book at Alec the Frog, resting comfortably in the dog crate on my dresser.

"You really know how to write a page turner, Alec," I said. "Most fantasies take forever before anything cool happens. And there's usually way too much description of every flower petal and article of clothing." I pretended to yawn. "Your story moves much faster. Your heroine is awesome."

I continued to read and discuss the passages in the book with the frog as though, at any moment, he might miraculously answer.

"Did you always want to be a writer?" I asked. The frog blinked. "I don't know why you waste your time working for my aunt if you're such a big deal author."

Marley poked her head in the doorway. "Mom, are you talking to the frog again?"

I tried to disguise my guilty expression. "Maybe."

"Aren't you supposed to be getting ready for your evening out?"

I frowned. "What time is it?"

"Quarter to eight," she replied. "Mrs. Babcock is downstairs with Starry Hollow Monopoly and a teabag."

"She knows I have tea here," I grumbled. "I don't know why she insists on bringing her own." I set the book on the bed. "I still need to get dressed. I got distracted by the book."

Marley laughed. "Now you sound like me. What are you reading?"

"Alec's book," I said. "I had it at the beach, remember?"

"I was riding my boogie board," Marley said. "For once, I wasn't paying attention to a book." She opened the inside front cover. "Who's Tatiana?"

"I don't know. Why?"

"He dedicated the book to her." Marley held up the dedication page that I'd skipped over.

For Tatiana.

"Maybe an old girlfriend?" I suggested. I hadn't heard her name mentioned in the office. I wondered whether it was the woman Linnea had mentioned. The one Alec and the sheriff had fought over years before. I'd have to dig around and find out.

"Is Ben picking you up?" Marley asked.

"No, I'm meeting him at his place so we can explore the parts of town I haven't seen yet. I need inspiration for the tourism board."

"You really need a car," Marley said.

"I'm aware of that. Aunt Hyacinth says she'll take care of it. In the meantime, walking is good exercise."

"Not when you're already running late," Marley replied.

I pinched her chubby cheek. "Stop making sense."

I quickly changed my clothes and ran a brush through my hair. I opted for comfortable shoes under the circumstances. It wasn't like I was interested in impressing Ben.

I blew a kiss at Alec the Frog and gave Marley a goodnight hug before hustling out the door.

"Don't forget to walk PP3 before bed," I called over my shoulder.

Although it was dark, there were so many fireflies blinking around me that I had no trouble finding my way to the main road. I knew it would be more convenient once I had a car, but I honestly didn't mind the walk into town. With the roar of the ocean in the distance and the nighttime serenade of the cicadas, it was downright heavenly to walk around in Starry Hollow in the evening. Even the stars seemed brighter here, probably because there was less air pollution. This place would still seem magical to me even without magic.

Without magic.

An image of Robina popped into my mind and I felt a pang of sympathy for the ex-criminal fairy. At least she managed to turn her life around by helping Ben establish his magical barbershop, although technically her fairy friend was responsible because Robina was banned from practicing magic. Ben's words flashed in my mind—*her magic changed my life...Mastermind.*

My breathing hitched as I passed by the library.

I checked the clock on my phone. Okay, I was late, but I could squeeze in a hot minute to stop by Robina's. She lived in Ben's building, after all.

I arrived at the apartment building and wiped the sweat from my forehead. I was pretty sure I had on enough deodorant to protect the entire Eagles football team, so the only smell emanating from me should be a soothing lavender.

Luckily for me, the occupants' names were listed on the mailboxes. Starry Hollow apparently had zero trust issues. It was both nice and unsettling. Robina's apartment was listed as 3E. I *had* to ask her. I knew I wouldn't be able to focus on anything else tonight if my mind was preoccupied with Robina.

I took the elevator to the third floor and easily located her apartment. I knocked on the door, my stomach knotting. For a brief moment, I debated calling the sheriff first. What if she turned out to be a raging maniac and I'd voluntarily put myself in her apartment?

I inhaled deeply and quickly calmed my nerves. No, I only had a simple question. What kind of journalist would I be if I was too scared to knock on the older fairy's door?

Robina answered the door with a ready smile. "Miss Rose, what a lovely surprise. Are you lost? Ben lives upstairs. He has the whole penthouse suite to himself, you know."

"You don't need to sell me on Ben," I said. "I'm here because I have a quick question for my investigation."

"Of course," Robina said, gesturing me inside. "What is it?"

I stepped into the modest apartment and noticed the sparse furnishings and impersonal artwork on the walls. It seemed like Robina had never really embraced the place as her own. Maybe it was her years in prison that made it diffi-cult to personalize the space.

"I've been thinking about the magic in Snips-n-Clips," I said. "What was the name of your fairy friend who infused it with magic?"

Robina clasped her hands together—a nervous gesture. "Josie."

"Josie what?"

"She's not local anymore," Robina said quickly. "She moved a few years ago."

"To where?"

"Cincinnati. She wanted to try the human world for a change."

"No one chooses Cincinnati as the place they want to live

in the human world," I said, folding my arms. "Robina, be straight with me. Are you the one responsible for the shop's magic?"

Guilt seemed to envelop her. "I was originally, but I haven't done magic in years. I swear. I only helped Ben set up the shop because I wanted to repay him for his kindness. If it weren't for him, I'd be unemployed and homeless."

"But how does the magic keep going if you don't do it?" I asked. "Don't the spells wear off?"

"Some do. Some don't."

I arched an eyebrow. "So how do you manage the ones that do if you're not practicing magic?"

She gave an exasperated huff. "I taught Ben how to do certain spells."

"But how?" I asked. "He's an elf. I didn't think they could do magic."

"In my experience, anyone can do magic with the right teacher," Robina said. "And Ben was a keen student."

"Robina, that could be considered a violation of your parole. You could go back to prison."

"I'm aware of that," she said. "There didn't seem to be a reason for anyone to know. He treats me like his own mother. I only wanted to help him."

"And did you also want to help him find a wife?" I asked. "Maybe you decided to take matters into your own hands and eliminate the competition?"

"No, no." She waved her hands excitedly. "I would never do that. Those frogs have nothing to do with me."

As much as I wanted to believe her, the evidence seemed stacked against her.

"I'm sorry, Robina, but I think I should call the sheriff," I said, and moved to retrieve my phone.

A voice behind me stopped me in my tracks. "You'll do no such thing."

I jerked my head toward the sound of Ben's voice. "Ben! How did you know I was here?" I asked.

"You're late, so I went to see if you'd gotten lost," he said. "You should know that your voice carries. You may want to work on your volume now that you've left New Jersey."

I cleared my throat. I *did* have a tendency to speak loudly.

"Why did you lie about Robina practicing magic?" I asked. "You're the one who told me a friend of hers helped you with the shop."

"Why do you think?" he asked. "To protect her."

I looked from Ben to Robina, the realization dawning on me. "And to protect yourself," I said quietly.

"Protect myself from what?" Ben queried.

"You didn't want the sheriff or me to know that you could do magic," I said. "Under normal circumstances, you'd have been proud of mastering a skill like that. I bet it's not easy for an elf."

His jaw tightened. "Put away your phone, Ember. I'm warning you."

"Turn them back," I demanded. "Turn the frogs back into men and I won't say a word."

"You won't say a word because you won't be able to speak," he said, advancing toward me.

"I don't understand," I said, stepping backward. "I usually read people pretty well. You seemed like a nice guy."

His eyes narrowed dangerously. "I *am* a nice guy. That's the whole problem. Don't you see? Day in and day out, I would wait on clients who were spoiled for choice when it came to the opposite sex. Meanwhile, I couldn't get any girl's attention. Do you know how many times I tried to gather the courage to ask out Dakota?"

I nodded in sympathy. "I hear you on that one. She's a real catch."

"And yet she was willing to try her luck with three of the

most notorious bachelors in town," he seethed. "Why do women fall all over themselves to be with guys like that? They come into my shop and boast of their conquests like these women are nothing more than slabs of meat. I would treat them like the goddesses they are. They deserve better."

I heard the pain of rejection in his voice and my stomach clenched. "But Dakota didn't reject you, if you didn't even have the courage to ask her out."

"She would've said no," he blurted. "How could I compete with those other guys? Florian lives in Thornhold and I live on the top floor of an apartment building."

"But it's the penthouse," I reminded him. "The whole top floor. And you *own* the building."

"It isn't enough," he said angrily. "I'm never enough."

"What about Alec? He didn't do any of the things you're accusing the others of. He didn't even go out with Dakota."

Ben fixed me with his hard stare. "No, but he certainly held your attention at Elixir. You were supposed to be on a date with me."

Someone had a serious case of the green-eyed monster. "To be fair, I didn't consider it a date," I said. "And I thought we had a nice time that evening."

"You had a nice time because you nearly had your tongue down Alec Hale's throat. I don't blame you, really. He's everything I'm not."

I didn't argue with that statement. "What was your plan, then? Turn every bachelor in town into a frog? Clear the decks so that you were one of the few options for all the single ladies in Starry Hollow?"

"Something like that," he mumbled.

"I can see how you managed to curse your clients," I said. "You had access to pieces of their hair from the barbershop. But how did you manage to curse Alec?"

"I went to his office to get my books signed. You weren't there at the time."

I nearly slapped my forehead. Of course. The books on Alec's desk belonged to Ben. *The Final Prophecy* I took from the office was part of Ben's collection.

"It was simple enough to pluck a stray hair from his expensive suit jacket." Ben smiled. "He even thanked me."

"And you rewarded his good manners by turning him into a frog," I said hotly. "What about Robina? The woman you consider to be a mother figure." I glanced at the wingless fairy, who stood silently in the corner, keeping a safe distance from us. "Don't you realize that you've endangered her?"

"The only way I've put her in an awkward situation is if someone discovers the truth," Ben said. "But that's not going to happen."

Fear gripped me as he reached for a strand of my hair. I smacked his hand away.

"Ouch," he cried.

"Did you think I was just going to let you take it?" I asked, my eyes blazing. "Do I look like a pushover to you?"

He inhaled sharply. "Fine then. We'll do it the hard way. I don't need your hair to curse you." He retrieved a wand from his back pocket. It was Barbie pink with glitter on the star at the end of the wand.

My eyes widened. "It really goes with your outfit," I said.

"It's my old wand," Robina said quietly. She seemed surprised to see it in Ben's possession.

"I thought your wand was taken away," I said.

"That's the one I trained with as a girl," she said. "I turned in my adult wand, but not that one. Every fairy gets a starter wand."

"How does no one notice a grown elf carrying around a sparkling pink fairy wand?" I asked.

"That's sexist," Ben said. "Anyway, I used a cloaking spell on it."

That made sense. If my father was able to use a cloaking spell on me to hide my location, then Ben could certainly use one on an object as small as a wand.

"Listen, you don't want to hurt me, Ben," I said. "It isn't worth it." As always, my first thought was of Marley. I couldn't let anything happen to me. At least this time, if something bad happened, she wouldn't be alone. She would have cousins to raise her. It was a small consolation.

"Bippety boppity," Ben began.

He pointed the wand in my direction. Before he could finish uttering his fairy phrase, I focused my will on the wand and tried pulling it toward me. It was heavier than a feather, but lighter than an apple. Thank goodness for practicing magic at Linnea's and Haverford House. The witches were right—it really was like exercising a muscle. The wand wiggled in his hand and the small movement gave me the confidence to continue. In my mind, I wrenched the wand free.

"To me," I yelled, and the wand shot into my outstretched hand.

Ben and I stared at the wand, equally shocked by the outcome.

"You're telekinetic," Robina whispered.

Ben stared at me, dumbfounded. "But you don't know how to do magic yet. You came from the human world." He looked ready to cry. I wouldn't have been the least bit surprised to see him stomp his foot next.

"You seem to forget one thing, Ben," I said, and pointed the wand back at him. "I'm Ember Rose, first of her name. Daughter of Nathaniel and Lily. Descendant of the One True Witch. Plus, I'm from New Jersey. My badassery knows no bounds."

Okay, maybe that declaration was overkill, but the power was coursing through my veins and there was no stopping it. I had no clue what to do with the obnoxious pink fairy wand, but I couldn't let Ben see me hesitate. I opened my mouth for a phony incantation when I remembered the fairy spell Tanya had used on Alec in the office.

"Super duper, Ben-in-stupor," I said, waving the wand.

Ben froze in place.

"That's excellent work for a beginner," Robina said from the corner.

I shot off a text to the sheriff and gave him the address.

"How long will the spell last?" I asked Robina.

"Long enough for the sheriff to arrive," she replied.

I eyed her carefully. "You're not going to try and stop me?"

She shook her head sadly. "No. A good mother knows when her child needs to learn a valuable lesson, especially a mother who's served time."

I gave her a sympathetic look. "Tough love is tough on everyone."

Robina nodded and crossed the room to stand beside me. "I didn't realize he'd become so jaded," she said. "I should've noticed. Some mother figure I am."

"Robina, don't beat yourself up. Ben probably hid it from you because he didn't want you to be accountable. Deep down, he didn't want you to get tangled up in this."

Robina heaved a sigh. "I suppose he cares for me in his own way."

I studied the frozen elf. "It's a shame, really. He seemed to have everything going for him, but he let his own feelings of inadequacy get in the way."

"Drop the wand and put your hands up," a familiar voice said.

I held the wand over my head as Sheriff Nash bolted into

the room. "Rose, for Nature's sake. What are you doing with that fairy wand?"

"This wand did the frog curses," I said, wiggling it. "Ben's the one you're after. I froze him for you."

"Froze him?" the sheriff queried.

I inclined my head. "Like an elf popsicle. Check it out." I flicked my fingers on Ben's arm. "Ouch. That actually hurt me."

The sheriff mangled a laugh before focusing on Robina. "You're sure Ben is the culprit? I assumed I was here to arrest Robina."

I shook my head. "You don't want her. Ben is solely responsible for this. She didn't know it was him."

The sheriff studied Ben. "Can you unfreeze him? It will make it easier to arrest him."

I bit my lip. "Um, I don't know how."

Robina raised her hand. "I can help her, Sheriff, if you want me to."

He stood with his hands on his hips, deciding. "Tell her what spell to do, but don't do it yourself."

Robina whispered the magic words and I channeled them through the wand. Ben's body jerked as he became unstuck. The sheriff wasted no time slapping a pair of glittering handcuffs on the elf.

"Why are your handcuffs bedazzled?" I asked.

"I have special handcuffs for certain paranormals," he explained. "These are my fairy handcuffs. It stops them from using their hands to do magic."

"But Ben is an elf," I said.

"An elf who knows fairy magic, apparently," Sheriff Nash said. "I'm not taking any chances."

I stared at the wand in my hand. "So can I reverse the curse with this wand?"

"I can help you with that, and the protection spell as well,"

Robina said. "Now that I know he used my old wand, I'm pretty sure I know the spell he performed. It's one that I learned as a young girl. He must've found my old school primer."

"In your closet," Ben admitted. "I found them both when I came to repair the shelf, remember?"

Robina pressed her lips together, her disappointment evident. "So you stole them?"

"I borrowed them," Ben said. "I always planned to return them."

"When? After I'd gone back to prison?" Robina asked. "Benjamin, your behavior has disappointed me greatly."

Ben hung his head in shame. "I'm sorry, Robina. I never intended for you to get caught up in any of this."

"Let's go, Ben," the sheriff said. "You'll have plenty of time to offer apologies from your prison cell."

"Won't you need the fairy wand as evidence?" I asked.

"Use it to reverse the curse first," he replied. "Then I'll log it in as evidence."

Once they left the apartment, Robina placed a grateful hand on my shoulder. "I don't know how to thank you. You could easily have thrown me under the broomstick. Why didn't you?"

"Because you're innocent. The only one who deserves the blame here is Ben," I said. "You put your trust in the wrong person. That isn't a crime."

Robina moved toward the kitchen. "Let me get my phone and I'll text you the spells you need to restore your cousin and the other gentlemen."

"Thanks, Robina," I said. "I guess your life just got a heck of a lot busier, now that you've got a barbershop to run single-handedly."

Robina's eyes widened. "I hadn't even thought of that." She clamped her hand over her mouth. "Goodness gracious. There will be a million things to do before tomorrow."

"And you'll manage them all without magic," I said. "I'm happy to persuade your customers not to leave once they hear the news about Ben. If I can convince Florian to stay, I bet a lot of others will, too."

"I'd appreciate that," she said, her thumbs moving on her phone at a rapid pace. "Despite what happened, I'm proud of what Ben and I built together. I don't want to be the one to destroy it."

My phone dinged as the text arrived. "You won't, Robina. You've taken your second chance to heart. That much is clear." I tucked the pink wand under my arm. "I'll see you around."

"Where are you off to now?" she asked.

I waved the phone in the air. "It's time to turn a bunch of frogs back into small town princes."

CHAPTER 17

LESS THAN AN HOUR LATER, I stood in one of the drawing rooms of Thornhold in front of a row of hopping frogs. I'd retrieved Alec from my bedroom, and Sheriff Nash had brought the others so we could change them all back at once. I had my fingers crossed that Florian was among them.

"How do I tell which one is which?" I asked. "The only one I can identify is Alec because of those adorable fangs."

"It doesn't matter," Aunt Hyacinth snapped. "Just get started." She'd insisted on being present when Florian was brought back into existence. I had the sense that she wanted to kiss him and box his ears at the same time.

I took Robina's wand and read her text message out loud, aiming at the first frog on the left. There was a sound that reminded me of a hissing firework and then an unfamiliar man appeared where the frog had just been. He looked around in a stupor, as though waking up from a long sleep.

"Cayden," Sheriff Nash said. "How do you feel, buddy?"

Cayden blinked. "Where am I? This place is super nice."
He wore what I assumed was the same outfit he'd been transformed in. Part of me had wondered whether they'd reap-

pear naked, like a shifter would. To my relief (but maybe a little disappointment), that wasn't the case.

"Of course it is, darling," Aunt Hyacinth said. "It's my home."

"We'll explain everything later," the sheriff said. "Right now, we need to restore the other men."

Thom Rutledge was next, and then Alec. The vampire seemed less confused, as though he knew exactly what had happened. Unfortunately, the last frog didn't budge.

"What's the problem?" my aunt demanded. "What's wrong with Florian?"

"Um, I'll tell you in a minute," I said, my stomach sinking. "Let's get these other guys squared away first."

"Welcome back, gentlemen," the sheriff said. "I've been told that you should drink plenty of water after a curse like this."

"Hydration is key," I added.

"Curse?" Thom queried. "What kind of curse? Why do my legs feel like they've been turned backwards?" He bent his knees and then kicked out his legs.

"We were turned into frogs," Alec said. "Please tell me you've apprehended that wretched elf."

"You knew it was him?" I asked.

"He came into my office with a few of my books to sign," Alec said. "It was the way he asked me about you. I realized in that moment, but it was too late. I don't think he even waited to leave the office before cursing me."

I gave the others the full recap of Ben and his jealous tendencies.

"He's in custody now," the sheriff said. "I arrested him earlier."

Alec studied me closely. "And whom do we have to thank for our restoration?"

"It was a group effort," I said. "It's a good thing we have experienced fairies like Robina on hand."

"Indeed," Alec said. He didn't seem to be buying the manure I was selling. Or the minotaur shit, as people in Starry Hollow liked to say. "Well, my gratitude to everyone involved." He bowed and my pulse accelerated. He really was the most elegant man I'd ever met.

"I started reading your book, by the way," I told him.

"And what do you think?"

"Not sure yet. I'm only a quarter of the way through it. For some reason, I've been busy with outside activities."

He straightened the ends of his sleeves. "You don't say."

The other men downed several glasses of water, and headed for their respective homes. Alec walked with me to the front door.

"Would you like me to escort you to the cottage?" he asked.

"It's only right here, and I need to go with my aunt to the pond in the woods to find Florian before she has a heart attack."

"An escapee?" He seemed mildly amused.

"I'd rather not elaborate."

"Is that why you took me home with you?" he asked. "To keep me from escaping into the woods?"

I hesitated. "I...just wanted to keep you safe."

Alec's expression softened. "Thank you for your concern." He inclined his head. "And you're wrong about the prince. His motives have yet to be revealed."

The prince? I suddenly realized he meant the prince in *The Final Prophecy*. "Wait, you could hear me?" Blazing glory. If he could hear me, that also meant he could see me. Heat crawled through my body.

A smile tugged at his lips. "And I do quite like the leopard undergarments you wore yesterday. Very flattering."

My breath caught in my throat. "You saw me half naked?"

He paused. "Not just half…"

My face drained of color. I'd changed in front of the frog. Several times. It hadn't occurred to me that he'd remember anything once the curse was broken. I really needed a primer on the basics of magic.

"Not to worry, Miss Rose," he said. "Trust me. You have nothing to be embarrassed about."

With those words, he moved at lightning speed and disappeared into the evening air.

Sheriff Nash and Aunt Hyacinth accompanied me to the pond. My aunt was less than thrilled to hear my confession about Florian.

"Marley only wanted him to feel more comfortable," I explained. "Then he hopped away and refused to come back."

"Sounds like my son," Aunt Hyacinth said bitterly. "Even in frog form, he's a thorn in his family's side."

Phew. At least she wasn't angry with me.

"What if he isn't here?" my aunt asked. "What if he's been eaten by a predator?"

"His survival instincts will be firmly intact," I said. "If any owls made a beeline for him, he'd duck underwater."

"He's Florian Rose-Muldoon," the sheriff added. "He always lands on his feet."

"True," my aunt said. She'd never argue with the distinguished luck of the Rose family.

When we arrived, three frogs occupied lily pads.

"Any inklings as to which one is Florian?" I asked, assuming one of them was.

They shook their heads.

"Then I'll just go ahead." I repeated the same spell that restored the other frogs to their true selves. The frog on the middle lily pad transformed into a man and promptly plunged into the water. I recognized Florian's white-blond head as it crested.

Aunt Hyacinth's laugh was deep and throaty. "Serves him right. Perhaps now he'll learn a hard lesson about his questionable dating habits."

"He didn't get cursed by one of his dates, though," I said. I doubted Florian would learn anything from this experience, except that maybe he enjoyed the taste of flies more than he expected to.

Florian dragged himself from the pond, his clothes dripping. He looked thoroughly confused.

"Did I stay out all night drinking again?" he asked, rubbing his head.

"No, darling." Aunt Hyacinth quickly gave him her version of a motherly embrace. It consisted of a hand on the arm and an air kiss next to the cheek. "You've been a frog."

His brow furrowed. "A frog? Well, that explains the constant buzzing in my ears." He whacked his right ear with his palm.

"We have the offender in custody," Sheriff Nash said. "Thanks in no small part to your cousin here."

Florian clapped me on the shoulder. "And here you thought you were lucky that we found you. I'm starting to think it's the other way around."

This week's paper dropped onto my desk and the first thing I noticed was my name in print. *The Curious Case of the Bachelor Frogs* by Ember Rose.

I glanced up to see Alec. "Congratulations on a well-deserved byline, Miss Rose."

"Thanks," I replied. I traced my name with my finger. "It seems weird to have my name on something other than an outstanding bill."

"It isn't fair," Bentley complained. "You had the sheriff helping you."

"I can't help it if he's always tagging along," I said dismissively. "The guy really needs a hobby."

Bentley stifled a laugh and I groaned.

"He's here, isn't he?" I asked, as Alec stepped aside to reveal the sheriff.

"He is," Sheriff Nash said.

"Hey there," I said weakly. "What brings you to our fine establishment?"

"Just checking on each of the victims for any lingering side effects." The sheriff cocked his head. "How about it, Alec? Craving any mosquitoes?"

"Mosquitoes do have a taste for blood, so I can see the attraction," Alec said, not taking the bait.

"The only one I haven't caught up with is Florian," the sheriff said.

At that moment, the office door opened and Florian sauntered in. The sheriff's mouth opened and closed.

"The sheriff wants to know if you're suffering from any side effects, Florian," I said.

"No. I'm good as new," Florian said. "Even have a second date scheduled with Dakota Musgrove."

My hand shot up to high-five him. "Good move, cousin. She's a keeper."

"What brings you here, Florian?" Alec asked.

"I came to see my superstar cousin," Florian replied.

Bentley leaned toward me. "He's speaking ironically, right?"

I ignored the grumpy elf's remark. "As you can see, I'm right here, Florian."

"Excellent. Come with me for a moment, if you will." Florian wiggled his fingers.

I followed Florian outside, where he leaned against a silver sports car. The keys dangled from his fingertips.

"You came all the way here to show me your new car?" I asked. That was...nice.

"Not my new car," he said, and handed me the keys. "*Your* new car."

I stared at the gleaming sports car in disbelief. It was the kind of car I used to repossess from entitled suburbanites locked in an arms-style race with their wealthier neighbor.

"My new car?" I repeated. "Florian, I can't afford this."

He shrugged. "I know, but I can. It's paid in full. Consider it a thank you."

I choked on my response. "Does your mother know?"

"She approved the budget. In fact, I expected to spend less." He opened the driver's door. "Want to take it for a spin?"

My feet were fixed to the ground. I couldn't believe this was my life now. A new family. Magic powers. A beautiful cottage and now a fancy car. The only thing missing was a...

"Nice ride," Sheriff Nash said, stepping beside me to admire the roadster.

Alec appeared on the other side of me. "Vintage, too. You do have exquisite taste, Florian. Not that I'm at all surprised."

"I'm going to call her Sylvia," I announced.

The men exchanged confused glances.

"What? Every car needs a name," I said. "People name boats. Why not cars?"

"You make a good point," Sheriff Nash said. "Go on. Give it a whirl. Watch your speed, though. Deputy Bolan is patrolling as we speak."

I definitely didn't want the feisty leprechaun to pull me over. For one thing, he'd enjoy it far too much.

I slid behind the wheel and sank into the soft leather. "I could fall asleep in this seat, it's so comfortable."

"I don't recommend falling asleep behind the wheel," Sheriff Nash said. "That's a guaranteed accident."

Florian hopped into the passenger seat. "Let's roll."

I closed the door and rolled down the window. "Be back in a few minutes, boss."

Alec gave me a crisp nod.

I hit the gas, giving Florian the shock of his life. Thankfully, Coastline Drive wasn't too busy, so I raced along the coast, admiring the ocean view as we went. A broomstick tour flew overhead and I waved out the window. We passed the spot for boat and kayak rentals, Balefire Beach, Mariner's Landing, Fairy Cove, the Lighthouse, and the Whitethorn—so many places that made Starry Hollow special.

"Where's the radio?" I asked. I panicked when I didn't see any controls.

"That's one of the magical parts," Florian said proudly. "Just say the song you want—any song—and it will play."

"Any song at all?" I queried.

"That's right."

Amazing. "Is there a Bluetooth button?" I asked, squinting at the screen.

"We use the Bluetooth Fairy here," he said, and pointed to a button of a sparkling blue tooth on the screen. "It's an old car, but completely restored."

"Can you pair it with my phone?" I asked.

Florian grinned and snapped his fingers. "I'm not opposed to technology, but magic is much more efficient."

"I need to make a quick call to Aster," I said. "I just had a couple of ideas for the town slogan."

"Great. What are they?" Florian asked.

"Come to Starry Hollow for all your magic moments," I said. "Or, come to Starry Hollow and fall under its spell."

He nodded. "I like both of those."

Me, too. In fact, I could think of a dozen more. "I've even got one that might appeal to you."

"Let's hear it," he said.

I smiled. "Come to Starry Hollow—where spells were made to be broken."

Florian laughed. "You just might be onto something, Ember." He pointed to the street sign. "Turn here. You can drive back into town and show off your wheels a little more."

I glanced at the clock. "You know what? I'll turn on Thistle Street. There's somewhere I'd like to go."

The truth was, there was only person I wanted to share my good fortune with, and she was due to leave school in ten minutes.

"Marley will love it," he said, understanding.

She would. I turned on Thistle Street, and headed toward the middle school.

"*Drive* by The Cars," I said loudly and clearly, and the soothing ballad began. I flashed Florian a bright smile.

Who's going to drive me home tonight, the singer wanted to know. That was easy. *I* was.

If you want to find out about new releases by Annabel Chase, sign up for my newsletter here: http://eepurl.com/ctYNzf

Starry Hollow Witches
Magic & Murder, Book 1
Magic & Mystery, Book 2
Magic & Mischief, Book 3
Magic & Mayhem, Book 4
Magic & Mercy, Book 5
Magic & Madness, Book 6

Spellbound
Curse the Day, Book 1
Doom and Broom, Book 2
Spell's Bells, Book 3
Lucky Charm, Book 4
Better Than Hex, Book 5
Cast Away, Book 6
A Touch of Magic, Book 7
A Drop in the Potion, Book 8
Hemlocked and Loaded, Book 9
All Spell Breaks Loose, Book 10

Made in the USA
Middletown, DE
02 December 2019

79820773R00118